CHILD OF NIGHT

Laynie Bynum

Midnight Tide
PUBLISHING

MIDNIGHT TIDE PUBLISHING

contents

For my wildflower.
May you grow, dance, and love with abandon for we are more
than the sums of our mental illnesses.
When the darkness comes, just call for me and I'll be there.

BLURBS

"Laynie has one hell of a talent that will make you become her character. If you read this book, prepare to leave your life behind because once you start page one, your life is no longer your own."
  -Goodreads Reviewer

"Dynamic characters and themes of the importance of family ties and friendship."
  —Destiny Constantin - Reedsy Discovery

"The concept of going back in time was super fun to see and have Avery interact with her ancestors instead of just learning about them in a book or something. The duality of the sisters' magic was really cool too!"
  -Reviewer

one

I knew better than to get comfortable here. But I'd let myself slip. As the rest of my class was leaving, I'd taken a moment lean against the windowsill and stare out at the cityscape. It was a simple gesture and for anyone else, anyone but me, it wouldn't have been anything to bat an eye at. I lingered too long, soaking in the view of Boston. Searching out the buildings I knew and reliving all the different car rides to and from different foster homes across the city. I didn't even notice my mistake until the biology teacher gasped. I spun around and took in her horrified expression, like a punch to the gut.

"What have you done?" she asked as she motioned back to the window.

For a moment I wondered if maybe I'd left fingerprints on the windowsill or something else entirely mundane, but as I followed her gaze, I saw them.

The Ficus plants in six different black plastic pots, which we're healthy and thriving when I walked up, were all limp and brown now.

"I... I didn't—" but she wasn't going to listen. I knew it even before she interrupted me. This wasn't the first time an accident had me at the mercy of a judgmental adult. Wrong place, wrong time, every time.

It wasn't like I meant to kill the plants, no matter what it looked like. Things like this just seemed to happen to me and I couldn't ever explain it. Plants died, fires started, things exploded. It would almost be comical if it wasn't so annoying.

Not even an hour passed before I found myself in the vice principal's office with my foster mom, Lynne, trying to convince both of them I was innocent. But without any evidence or an explanation for what might have happened, there was no way I could charm my way out of this.

"What did you use? Bleach? Something stronger? Where did you get it?"

The questions from Mrs. Curry were getting more and more accusatory with every moment, drilling into me with a practiced precision.

"I didn't kill them. I didn't do anything to them."

"You'd been jealous of that experiment ever since it was picked over yours for exhibition at the science fair. Just admit it, Avery. Admit it and we can move on with this meeting."

"I didn't do anything wrong. I was just staring out of the window. They must have been dead when I walked up."

She nodded but didn't speak. Her eyes bored into me from the other side of her desk as Lynne fidgeted uncomfortably with her purse strap. The vice principal's silence now was part of the mind game. I was sure of it. She was trying to break us.

I stared back defiantly from my chair. I'd done nothing wrong and I wasn't going to be blamed for it. Weird stuff happened to me all the time; that didn't mean I was trying to sabotage the experiment or whatever she was accusing me of.

I'd been here a whole year without getting kicked out, nearly twice as long as most of my other schools. That was totally a win in my book. And I didn't intend to stop the streak now. I'd do whatever it took to stay with Lynne, to stay here, as long as I could.

You would think that someone at this school would have seen how hard I'd been trying. That they'd notice my straight A's or the way I always did what I was told. Maybe instead of always laying blame on me, Curry could set me up with some of the nice crap the school gave other students with 4.0 GPAs.

It wasn't that they didn't care about the students. It wasn't like they didn't notice the other kids who got good grades. I mean just the week before Roland Bennett got an entire page in the school newspaper for his elementary school level biology project I was accused of destroying. But, of course, my own project about the thousands of bacteria in the human stomach was completely overlooked.

"We could expel her for this, you know." The wicked witch of Fenway High finally spoke, her thin lips pulled tightly against her teeth as if it pained her not to outright expel me right then.

Lynne stopped messing with her purse and looked up. "There's no need for that. I'm sure it was an accident."

Curry crossed her arms and tapped one long fingernail against her bicep. "Killing one ficus plant, maybe. But killing eight in various stages of growth? That was not an accident."

To Lynne's credit, she didn't shrink under the vice principal's heavy stare. "Avery's been moved around enough. As a fellow child advocate, I—"

Curry raised an eyebrow which made Lynne stop in her tracks, a rare moment of what looked like insecurity flashing across her face.

I reached over and squeezed her hand in solidarity, and after meeting my eyes for a second, she tried again. "I think it's best to keep her in a stable environment as long as possible. Developing a daily schedule of normality is important for foster children. Changing schools again would disrupt that. Is there some other punishment that would be fitting? Maybe she could help the janitor around school or have after-school detention."

Those sounded like horrible punishments for something I didn't even do. Plus, with my luck, I would end up headfirst in a garbage can or with a Breakfast Club level teacher for detention.

Rolling her eyes and lifting her desktop calendar's top page, Curry sighed. "We could bar her from attending the field trip next month to Salem, but I feel like with her attitude it may do her some good to get scared straight."

"What attitude?" I blurted out. Sitting there quietly, behaving, and minding my own business was hard enough without getting lectured and being told I was doing the opposite. If I was going to catch hell, it might as well be for something I was actually doing.

She raised one eyebrow at me and then looked at Lynne. "Point proven. She will spend every Saturday until the field trip helping the janitor paint the bathrooms."

Lynne smiled at Curry as if we had just received the best plea deal we could have hoped for when in reality it was bull.

"*And*," Curry continued after a moment, "she will work with Roland Bennett to help him replace the months' worth of work she destroyed."

I threw my head back and groaned. Painting bathrooms was heaven compared to having to work with that blowhard. The school revered him as if he was a saint and he let it go to his head. He was constantly the first in class with his hand up to answer a question, always the first to volunteer to help or go the extra mile for the teachers. He made it entirely impossible for anyone else in that school to get noticed in his shadow. Sure, he'd never done anything to me personally, but just having to exist in the same space as him was enough of a buzzkill.

Lynne nodded vigorously as she stood up, grabbing her purse with one hand and my closest hand with the other. "Thank you, Mrs. Curry. She will."

We stepped out into the hallway, and I pulled my hand away from hers. "What was that, Lynne? I thought you we're going to stand up for me. This whole thing is just so unfair."

"Did you want to be expelled? Do you really think if you were the state wouldn't move you to another foster home?"

I looked away from her, out of the tall glass windows lining the hallway. "I *want* to not get punished for things I didn't do."

She lowered her head as she looked at me indignantly. "They said you touched the plants and they died. Can you explain that?"

I slid my hand across my face in exasperation. "If I could, I would have before she handed down my death sentence."

Lynne walked out of the front doors and started to the minivan. I took a deep breath before I followed her, watching her micro braids swish back and forth like pendulums in the Boston breeze. "A few days of painting won't hurt you, Avery."

The sky rumbled overhead and I could almost smell the incoming storm that would soon be looming above us. The weather had a way of matching my mood perfectly and right then my mind was a hurricane of indignant anger.

I opened the passenger side door as petulantly as possible and climbed in as Lynne turned the key in the ignition. "It's not the painting I'm worried about."

She had the audacity to laugh. "Some social interaction won't kill you either."

"You obviously don't know Roland Bennett."

★ ★ ★

"Mommy bought pizza," Olivia yelled excitedly as we walked in the door. Lynne handed a twenty-dollar bill to the court-approved babysitter who looked more than ready to escape.

Alison's auburn, unruly mane popped around the corner at the top of the stairs to verify the claim. She lazily set her book on the railing and shuffled down the stairs and into the small kitchen.

As she walked past our littlest foster-sister, she leaned down and chided under her breath, "Don't call her that."

Her voice was barely above a whisper, but since Ali was always so soft-spoken, it was hard to tell whether it was to avoid hurting Lynne's feelings or not.

"Why not? She looks like a mommy. She acts like our mommy. Why can't I call her Mommy?"

Lynne's back was to the table as she stood over the stove, evenly separating the pieces and putting them on paper plates, but her shoulders grew rigid, and her hands stilled. "You can do whatever makes you feel comfortable, Olivia. But Alison and Avery don't call me mommy and you don't have to, either."

She turned around with a smile and put the plates in front of each of us at the table.

The talk of parents must have been getting to Alison. Her head hung lower than normal as she picked at the pepperonis on her pizza. "Can I eat in our room?" she asked as stopped messing with her food and stood up.

I groaned as Lynne nodded. "Do not drop pizza grease on my bed. It's bad enough when you get crumbs all over it," I told her.

Alison stuck out her tongue and fled while Lynne grabbed a wet washcloth and wiped the pizza sauce off Olivia's mouth and sent her to brush her teeth for the night. "I wanted to talk to you about something while the little ones aren't around."

That was never a good sign. I'd had *talks* plenty of times. They usually ended with me heading to another group home to await another poor, unsuspecting foster parent. "If it's about school, I told you, I didn't do anything."

"It's not about that." She shook her head and looked up. "I—" she stalled. "I want to make some changes around here and I need your help."

Her cell phone began to ring and she looked frantically around for her purse. I took advantage of the momentary distraction to bolt from the room and head upstairs.

I couldn't put off the talk about kicking me out forever, but maybe I could for at least the night. After the day I'd had, I just wanted to sleep in my comfy bottom bunk one more time.

I climbed under my warm comforter and tried like hell to memorize the way the plush mattress felt against my bones, the creak of the wooden bunk beds as Alison tossed and turned above me, the sound of Lynne's footsteps as she walked up the stairs and into her room. I wanted to absorb every sensation I'd never get to experience again.

I'd never had a real home. Never had real parents. I had no clue who the people who birthed me even were. According to the different case workers who juggled me around over the years, they didn't either.

Olivia and Alison had been with Lynne for a most of their lives. They knew what it felt like to belong somewhere. I was the newest recruit, so to speak. Lynne was the latest in a long line of foster parents who had no clue what to do with me. It never took long before my anger and bad luck merged to make me into a destructive monster that destroyed their precious furniture or killed their carefully pruned bushes. It never mattered that I didn't actually do the things they accused me of, just like with Curry. What mattered was that I was a troubled kid with a rap sheet a mile long and their treasured possessions were ruined. That was enough to throw an eight-year-old back into the system apparently.

This was the first place where I could let myself relax. Lynne was the first foster mom I could ever trust. It was the first time I'd ever felt as if I could unpack my backpack without worrying that I'd never see those clothes or belongings again.

It didn't come easy, this sense of security. It wasn't overnight by any means. I'm surprised Alison didn't murder me for having to sleep with the lights on and being so protective over my clothes and other belongings that I'd pile them up on my mattress and sleep next to them. I had to have been a terrible roommate for those first few months.

There were so many times I thought it was the end, that I thought Lynne would kick me to the curb, but she always took the time to talk through them and gave me the benefit of the doubt. I'd never met an adult like that. Never known someone so patient.

Despite being certain that I'd drove her to her limit with my latest fiasco, when I woke up the next day, Lynne didn't even mention our postponed talk. In fact, days passed, and nothing was said. I'd go to sleep each night trying to soak up the small comforts this home had brought me, thinking it would be my last but, aside from some side-glances, life with Lynne continued as normal. Or as normal as possible.

All worries about potential drama at home ceased to exist as Roland Bennett became my main headache. I didn't actually kill his plants, but he could have at least acted like it was some sort of inconvenience. Instead, it was as if it was the excuse he needed to work on something else.

"Your project on gut germs was pretty cool. We could do something like that again," he said as we sat in the empty biology classroom after school.

His positivity was annoying. You'd think he had no where he'd rather be than trapped in school after-hours with a relative stranger.

I looked at him from the corner of my eye. "I'd say thank you, but I know you're lying. I doubt you even paid any attention to my presentation. You knew you were going to win no matter what I came up with."

"No, honestly. I had no clue all of that was going on in here." He grabbed his flat abs with both hands and pinched the bit of skin around them.

I faked a smile. "Yeah, well, your project is the one that made headlines. So, you should come up with the next one and just tell me what I have to do."

He scratched at his light brown curls. "Whatever. The judges like basic. That's why the plant experiment worked.

Things that are easy to understand for adults who have been out of school for a long time."

That explained why they wouldn't even look twice at mine. "You're the genius here. What's the easiest thing we can do then?"

He tapped his pencil against the desk like a drumstick and I held in a shudder of annoyance.

"Since you have a knack for killing things—"

"Not cool."

He winked at me and started over. "The last project was about how music affects growth. What if we did how music affects decomposition? We could use the same plants I started with even though they're dead now."

"So, what? We blare metal music at some and leave the others alone?"

He stood up, apparently inspired. "Think bigger, Avery. One genre for each plant. Classical music, pop, country." His hands dotted each of the words as if they were fireworks exploding across the air in front of my face.

I looked over at the plants lined up along the window. Sure, they were dead, but not like super dead and falling apart. "How long is this going to take?"

"That's the beauty of this experiment. We have no clue." His voice was nearly sing-song with happiness at the thought.

I pushed my palms against my eyes and then looked up toward the ceiling. "Why me? Seriously, couldn't you pick on anyone else?"

Roland, who was studying his plants, turned around. "What?"

"Not you, dipstick."

He looked from side to side at the empty classroom and waved his arms back and forth to silently ask who else I could be talking to.

"Just asking the universe why it felt the need to stick me here with you when I could be doing anything else in the world right now with literally anyone else."

He wiggled one heavy eyebrow. "Even Curry?"

I held my hands up in surrender. "Oh god, no. Not Curry. Anyone is better than Curry, even you."

"I'll take that as a compliment."

The switch from his old experiment to the new one was easy enough. So easy, I didn't see why I was needed at all. All we did was turn music on and wait. And wait. And wait.

Roland made a spreadsheet to keep up with the stages of decomposition and one of us checked on the plants every day. Aside from that, we stayed out of each other's way.

No. That's a lie.

I tried to avoid him, and he stopped me between every class to update me on the progress, scheduled after school meetings for us to analyze the data, and even convinced our science teacher that we needed to skip out on our normal lessons to work on our presentation.

There wasn't a lot of actual work that went on in these meetings, more just Roland rambling about how amazing decomposition was and how we should do more experiments together while I sat and pretended to listen.

Since arriving at Fenway High, this was the most interaction I had had with any of the other students. My reputation preceded me and if kids weren't scared of me, they made fun of me instead. Out of all the schools I'd been to, it wasn't the most stuck up, but it wasn't the most welcoming either. The teachers were as bad as the kids, their minds already made up about who I was before I entered the classroom. No matter how hard I worked or what expectations I exceeded, I was the juvenile delinquent foster kid with behavioral issues my file made me out to be.

If it hadn't been Roland Bennett, it wouldn't have been half bad either. I could tolerate the constant boasting and acting like he was the most intelligent person on earth, if I hadn't been so annoyed at the fact that his intelligence was celebrated while mine was looked over. He was the golden boy, probably with this perfect middle class family and a mom named Karen and I... wasn't. That was the only difference. I tried just as hard, knew just as much, got the same grades. But the difference between us was as stark as night and day.

Even if I wanted to let myself make friends with Roland, I knew better. It wouldn't be long before my life turned upside down once more and leaving behind friends always made it harder.

TWO

We managed to squeeze a semester's worth of work into the next month. At the end of it, we actually had something decent to show at the science fair. For the first time in my life, my knack at unfettered destruction had come in handy. The Ficus trees all decayed quite nicely under our care, just as we were hoping. And we had the science to back up why. Or most of it. I still wasn't able to explain how I killed them to begin with. I was just glad Roland didn't ever ask.

It was stupid. I shouldn't have been as excited for the science fair as I was. But the thought of finally being recognized for something was too sweet to ignore. My body buzzed with electric energy as we got ready to go. I was bringing my entire motley crew, all the fosters and Lynne.

It wasn't a rarity, us being together like this. We always went together to Olivia's dance recitals or Allison's spelling bees, but I'd never had anything to take them to. It was finally my turn.

"We're going to be late," I said as I waited at the front door for Lynne to finish tying Olivia's shoes.

Lynne grabbed the small child in her arms and threw her oversized purse onto her opposite shoulder. "We're moving as fast as we can." She turned to the stairs as she crossed the threshold. "Alison, get down here. We're leaving."

"I'm coming," Alison yelled down the stairs. "Just one more minute."

Lynne rolled her eyes and walked out to the minivan to buckle Olivia into her booster seat, a contraption I'd never been able to figure out.

I looked between the minivan in the driveway and where Alison's voice came from up the stairs before relenting. We were never going to get out of here if I didn't force Ali to leave. She was a homebody from the word go. More comfortable sitting at home and reading than interacting with the world around her.

"What are you doing?" I asked as I rounded the corner to our shared bedroom.

Alison sat on my bunk, her head in her hands and my clothes on her body. The ripped black skinny jeans were unbuttoned and her little pooch of chub hung out over them. My favorite ratty, old Nirvana t-shirt was stretched out over her top half, but way too long. She basically looked like she tried to copy my every day uniform, lacking only my purple pendant necklace and black combat boots.

I cautiously sat down on the bottom bunk and put my arm around her. She tensed under my touch. Touch wasn't a thing we did. I wasn't comfortable with it and neither was she, but I thought maybe it was what she needed at that moment.

She looked up at me and raised a brow. "Seriously, a hug?"

"I don't know, I thought maybe I'd try something different."

Alison looked at my arm as if it was a snake slithering around her shoulders. "Stick to yelling at me or brooding. It's what you do best."

I ground my teeth together as I surgically removed my arm from her shoulders. This was what I got for trying to help, a snarky kid in my face. "If you make me late for the science fair, I swear to God."

"See, that's the Avery I know," she said as she got up.

I crossed my arms and glowered back at her. "Why were you even wearing my clothes?"

She ruffled through the three-drawer dresser with stickers all over it that she had claimed as her own. "It's my first time going to the high school. I'll be there in two years, ya know? I wanted to make a good impression."

I laughed and her expression became guarded as if she thought I was making fun of her. "No, I'm not laughing at you. It's just, dressing like me would be the worst impression you could make. They hate me."

Alison rolled her eyes as she pulled out her own plain colored t-shirt and a pair of khakis and started to redress. "That's in your head."

I stood up and pointed to the door, more than ready to get out of the house and away from this awkwardness. "Come on, you're starting to sound like Lynne."

Hopping with one shoe on and the other in her hand, Alison followed me out. "She's smart though. She knows what she's talking about."

Maybe that was true, but if I'd learned anything from my fifteen years in the foster care system, it was that you didn't let yourself fall for the hokey mind control crap. I stalled on the bottom stair to respond to Alison. "She's paid to tell us stuff like that. It's her job."

Alison's voice was softer when it came a split second later. "Yeah, I guess you're right." I turned around to look at her and her deflated expression would have broken my heart, if I let myself feel things like that. Call me hardened or a brat, but I'd had my heart broken one too many times to even pretend to care about people anymore.

It wouldn't be long, and I'd be out of the door again to some other foster care family. With some other foster siblings. At another school. With another set of problems.

I just didn't have it in me to get attached again, to leave kicking and screaming while begging to stay. This time I'd walk away with my head held high. There would be no empty promises of keeping in touch, no BS pinky promises to never forget each other.

People like me didn't get the luxury of remembering. Not when remembering made you feel like you were drowning in the weight of your own losses and your own failures.

So instead, I sucked up my feelings, stuffed them deep down, and got into the van. Fifteen minutes late was almost a win for us. I'd expected to be much later with the way things went in our house. There was always some emergency that needed to be solved before we walked out of the door.

Thankfully, the drive to Fenway went by quick. Lynne parked outside of the gym and I threw open the van's sliding door, running as fast as I could to the spot inside where Roland had set up our experiment earlier in the day.

He looked up from one of the dead plants as I came to a screeching halt in front of him, my foster sisters trailing behind me like a train of misfit children following the lead engineer screwup. "You finally decided to show up."

"My fault," Alison said between gulps of air beside me. She was doubled over, her hands on her knees and her red hair bobbing up and down with her heavy breaths.

Roland seemed to notice my foster sisters for the first time and his face lit up. He looked between the three of us, probably trying to find some tiny bit of resemblance. But there was none to be had. Olivia was so pale and blonde. Alison's freckled skin and huge puff of hair stood out in any crowd. I was constantly tan, despite the moonglow I was hoping to achieve by staying inside most of the time. My jet-black hair hung in a bob around my chin and my lavender eyes set me apart from everyone, much less my foster family.

As Lynne walked up behind us, the cogs behind Roland's eyes kept turning, but appeared to come up empty handed as he blinked twice and extended his hand to shake hers. "You must be Mrs. Smith."

Lynne looked between me and him, sizing up the situation. Her last name wasn't Smith. She wasn't my mom. She wasn't even a Mrs. But admitting all of that on a first meeting would have been complicated, and I think she knew that. "Just call me Lynne," she said as she took his hand and gave it a brisk shake.

Olivia pulled on the leg of his jeans, and he looked down at her. "Hi there."

"I'm Olivia Laryn Bailey. But you can call me Livy because it's a lot to say."

Roland glanced up at me and then stooped on his knees so he was face to face with her. "I'm Roland Bennett. You can call me Roland," he said as he shook her hand as if she was an adult.

Olivia evaluated him with cautious eyes and I almost pulled her away on instinct. There was no telling what was going to come out of her mouth. "Why do you look kind of like Lynne but kind of like me?"

And there it was.

"Olivia!" I shouted as I took her hand and yanked her a couple of inches back from Roland. Lynne said Olivia's bluntness was because of her age and her curiosity, but this was taking it too far. No one ever asked her why she looked like a ghost even in the middle of summer; why would she think it was acceptable to ask someone else why they looked the way they did?

Roland laughed and shook his head. "No, it's okay, Avery. I've got this. You'd be surprised how often people ask."

Warily, I let go of Olivia's hand and let her walk back over to where Roland was still stooped near the table holding our experiment.

He held out his arm and rotated it back and forth, letting her get a good look at his skin. "My mom looks like you. My dad looked like Lynne. So, I'm like the swirl in between."

Lynne smiled a sweet smile that told me she picked up on the same thing I did — describing his father in the past tense.

Olivia's eyes were alight with curiosity, and I was scared of what was going to come out of her mouth next. "Sometimes I mix my ketchup with my mustard when I eat corn dogs. So, like that?"

"Kind of. Only I don't think I taste as good as muchup."

Olivia bounced on her tiptoes. "I like that word."

Someone more emotional might have been moved by how sweet they were together. But I was tired of the obvious games. I was here to win the science fair, not to let Roland get all buddy buddy with my foster family.

"Did the judges come by yet?" I asked as I pretended to make the already straight poster board even straighter.

He stood up and turned to face me. Olivia scrambled back behind Lynne's tall legs once his attention was off her. "Nope, I think you're just in time. Jordan's totally unoriginal volcano project exploded in their faces so they're running a bit behind. I'll never understand how someone can screw up something so basic."

I turned one of the potted plants about a quarter of an inch and then back again. "Because he's an idiot with the attention span of a squirrel."

It was true. It was true of most people in my grade. I thought it was true about Roland before he surprised me over the past month.

Roland shrugged his shoulders and seemed to accept my word as truth. "Fair enough."

Mrs. Curry, looking like a cross between a crow and the Swamp Thing, crossed the gym floor after examining the exhibit in front of us. The principal, Mr. Johnston, followed close behind her. It was clear, as it almost always was, that Curry was running the show. Johnston was just her lapdog. Her sidekick. I could only hope Curry's affinity for Roland would be enough to dilute her hatred for me and give us a fighting chance at winning.

She hummed and hawed as she looked over our findings on the poster board. "Seems Roland was able to recover the experiment you destroyed." Turning to him and speaking under her breath, she gave him a nudge with her elbow. "Good job, young man."

As if I had nothing to do with it. As if she wasn't the one who assigned me to work on it with him. A hot streak of pain and anger surged up my spine. It was as if the wind had been pulled from my lungs. Everything I'd been hoping for, longing for, was ripped out from underneath me like a magician pulling a tablecloth.

All those afternoons spent working on this project wiped away with one statement. All the pride that I'd built up against my will, piece by piece, as the experiment came together. Everything was just gone. Stolen from me by someone who had no right to take it.

Something in the utility closet behind us let out a mechanical sounding groan. Everyone in the auditorium turned to look. The metal doors normally locked shut so that mischievous teens couldn't vandalize anything, flew open and a wave of water the size of a miniature tsunami came flooding out, soaking everyone within a ten-foot radius.

Adults screamed as the flood of water soaked their expensive leather loafers and high heels. Kids began to sob as the water knocked over their tables and ruined their displays.

Somehow, I couldn't help but feel responsible. This was the kind of thing that always seemed to happen to me. It was my terrible luck in action.

I covered my face with my hands and tried to breathe. It was all too much. The screaming and running. The pain of Mrs. Curry's words still burrowing into my mind as they mixed with the shame and embarrassment of causing such a scene–even if no one else knew it was my bad luck that caused it.

The two senior administrators forgot about our experiment all together and ran over to profusely apologize, likely trying to avoid being sued. They promised towels and ushered the angry, confused crowd into hallways to calm them down.

As we watched them disappear through the gym doors, Roland held out his arms as his eyebrows climbed up nearly to his hairline. "That was weird."

He didn't know the half of it. This was tame compared to the things that normally happened to me. "Yeah," I said, but it sounded like a sigh.

"I don't even know if they liked our project or not."

It was a lie. He knew. Curry had confirmed as much.

"Me either," I lied back.

In the end, my fears of dragging Roland down were moot because once the flood was cleaned up and the winners were announced, he took home first place.

Yeah, that's right. Roland and only Roland won the prize. They didn't even call my name. When Lynne approached Mr. Johnston, livid with rage, he said it must have been an oversight and promised he would correct it. "I'm sure we can find another ribbon somewhere."

As if the ribbon was what I was worried about. Not that maybe, for once, I just wanted to be acknowledged for the good I did instead of only the bad. Maybe I wanted to be seen as the person I hoped to be rather than the one they pretended I was.

As soon as Johnston walked away, someone tapped my shoulder. I turned around to find Roland, holding his ribbon out to me. "Take it. You deserve it."

I narrowed my eyes at him. "I don't need your pity."

He shoved it forward again, insistent. "You won it fair and square. It's not like I need it."

Yeah, because he probably had a hundred more just like it at home. Must be nice to be the prized student, to receive what you earned.

"I don't *need* it, either," I sneered.

He backed up slowly. "I'm going to leave it on our table, and if it's gone when I come back, that's fine." He turned and started toward the gym doors before I could form a rebuttal.

"Yeah, well, there won't be any questions to ask because it will still be there," I called out to him.

Roland brought out the six-year-old playground bully in me. He frustrated me so much I could only think of elementary-level insults.

With most of the attendees ushered out because of the flood and the rest gone as soon as the winner was declared, the gym was nearly empty aside from my little crew of misfits. We were left with only bare tables and the clack of Olivia's shoes as she ran in circles as Lynne tried to cheer me up. "*You* know you did a good job. You don't need a ribbon to prove it."

More words she was paid to say. More generic lies to make me feel better.

"Let's go," I said instead of acknowledging her fake sentiment.

"Are you sure?"

I started walking to the door, knowing it would be enough of a response. As we passed our table, the glisten of the gold ribbon against the gray plastic table leapt out at me. Seeing it brought on another wave of jealousy-based nausea. He really did it. He really left the ribbon on the table where any one could take it.

That's how little he cared about it.

Well, I wasn't going to take it either. For all I cared, the janitor could chuck it with the rest of the day's trash. Although it was severely wounded, I still had some pride left. Hand me down prizes no one else thought I earned were nothing more than a waste of time and energy. I wasn't falling for it this time. It would always be the Roland Bennett show and no cheap bit of fabric was going to change that. I would forever be Avery Smith, the screw up. No matter how much effort I put into changing it. No matter what I accomplished.

All I wanted to do now was go home and bury my head into my pillow. I wouldn't cry. I learned long ago that tears never solved anything. But in my bed, I could at least collapse into the weight of sadness without prying eyes trying to convince me I was okay.

But, of course, nothing was ever easy for me. We couldn't just walk out of the door and get to the van in peace. We had to walk out to a massive thunderstorm where there had been a sunny sky a few hours before.

"Strange," Lynne said as she tried to pull me in for a hug that I skillfully dodged. "The forecast said it was supposed to be clear tonight. I didn't even bring an umbrella."

We all ran to the van, Lynne climbing inside and folding her long, slender body into the middle seat so she could buckle Olivia in. Once she climbed around to the driver's seat, she looked at me pointedly and opened her mouth to start in on some more child psychology head shrinking crap.

"Don't. Just don't," I said before she could get anything out. Her face fell but she closed her mouth. We drove home in silence. All of us were wet, cold, and miserable. Life was better when I didn't expect anything and now that the science fair was over, I could go back to my standard programing of fighting off bad luck and avoiding negative attention.

Three

N early an entire month went by after the science fair, and the subsequent end to my partnership with Roland. But there he was, next to me on the bus to our Salem field trip. It would have been easy to convince myself that I was the drama between the two of us. That constantly living in his shadow, despite being just as smart and just as capable, caused a deep-seeded jealousy to color my opinion of him. But then he did things like steal my phone and take ridiculous selfies of himself with it and all doubts vanished.

"Give me back my phone, you sea urchin," I growled at him.

He moved the phone high up in the middle of the aisle, way out of my reach. "Well, Avery, if you can't tolerate marine creatures, maybe you should change seats."

I silently cursed Lynne for stopping for coffee on the way to school. We'd been late because of her addiction to iced nonfat caramel macchiatos and the constant chaos that was our house. Five minutes earlier and I could have had my pick of cracked pleather seats to spend a miserable half hour in. Instead, I was stuck here dealing with this crap. I took a deep breath and tried to imagine what it would be like if Lynne and I had enough money to buy me my own car next year, but each agonizing moment with Roland reminded me that scenario was impossible.

From the second I stepped on the bus, Roland made it clear that he was not going to change seats. Even if I wanted to, there was no one who would let me sit beside them to get away from him — no friends or allies willing to step up and offer their seat. Apparently, knowing that I was stuck with him, he decided to be even more annoying than normal.

Being face to face with Roland always triggered my worst feelings of inadequacy and bitterness. This kid, this "golden child," was given every opportunity in life I was stripped of, and it didn't even phase him. Somewhere under the sweet, goofy guise he put on for everyone else, there had to be a spoiled, ungrateful darkness. I'd met kids like him before. The kind that pretends to be your friend then steal your clothes out of your gym locker, so you have to wear your sweaty uniform the rest of the day. Kids that smile to your face and then get together in little groups and tear apart everything you do because you're different or you don't have as much money as them. I'd had one too many foster siblings be just as friendly as Roland and then try to steal everything I had to my name.

Kids like that were toxic in the way sunlight was toxic. Slowly poisoning you while you think you're having fun. If I put my guard down for one moment, one sliver of a second, he would use me for all I was worth and discard me like the trash he thought I was.

It was the worst field trip in the history of field trips even before he stole my phone.

I lunged for it again, my entire upper half crossing over him, and the antique pendant hanging from my necklace clanked against his forehead. He grimaced and rubbed the offending spot as I stole my phone back and smugly celebrated my victory.

As if he'd never seen it before, which was possible even though I wore it every day, Roland eyed my necklace with curiosity. "What even is that thing?"

I glared at him and turned my entire body toward the window, making it clear that he was not going to get an answer. The fact that it was the only possession I had from my birth family was not something he needed to know.

I'd become quite adept at avoiding that conversation over the years.

Different cities. Different people. Always the same old unlovable, damaged Avery.

Whatever. All I had to do was sit here without killing the boy for a few more minutes. The signs for our first stop, the Salem Wax Museum, were up ahead. I started gathering my things and waited for the bus to stop. When it did, kids in the front rows started to disembark but Roland stayed seated.

"You're on the outside so you have to get out before me," I said with a sign. Sometimes as it was as if he felt so entitled that he didn't have to observe any sort of social etiquette.

"Go ahead. I want to be the last off the bus."

I couldn't tell if he was serious or just messing with me. "Why? Just to be problematic?"

"I don't know. I just like it better in the back of the crowd."

"You are the most infuriating person I have ever met," I huffed as I awkwardly crawled over his extended legs to get out, surrendering the fight. My battles with Roland were many, and I had to choose wisely which ones I wanted to waste my effort on. This was not one of them.

I caught up with the rest of my class as they walked waited for the tour guide to meet them outside of the entrance. No one noticed I was lagging behind, which was pretty normal. The cemetery beside us and the stained-glass witches on the windows next door gave me the creeps. The eerie weather didn't help. The sky was overcast like it might rain soon. The spotty bits of sun that worked through the clouds cast shadows from the nearby trees and statues onto the surrounding buildings. I could imagine the residents of the graves evicting their final resting places and coming for me at any minute.

"Spooked?" Roland's voice boomed behind me, and he jabbed his pointy fingers into my sides.

I jumped and struggled to regain my composure. "I'm fine," I lied. "This whole place is just super cheesy."

"What did you expect? Broomsticks and cauldrons? You do realize that the actual witch trials were less about magic and more about political aggrandizing and mob mentality, right?"

My eyes rolled back so far in my head I could almost see my brain. The tour guide herded the class into the building like livestock. The whole thing felt as if we were walking into a bad horror movie. We were led down narrow hallways filled with wax figures behind glass display cases while she recited the plaques from memory.

Roland continued his inane chatter into my ear the entire time. "It's all quite sad when you think about it. Some of these people were our age or younger. A lot of them were upstanding citizens."

"So, it would be better if they were actual witches?" I countered, less interested in his answer than making him feel like an idiot. "Like, if they practiced some sort of old, mystical religion, their murders would be justified?"

"Not what I meant, Aves, and you know it."

"Do I though, Ro?" He didn't know me well enough to give me a nickname. I wanted him to see how it felt, and no one I knew called him Ro.

"Ro. I like it," he said smugly. "Good deal. Now we have nicknames for each other."

So, that one backfired. Sinking to his level was exhausting.

Despite the overcrowded hallway, the air inside the museum was cold and I rubbed my arms against the beratement of the air conditioning.

Roland's hands went to the bottom of his black hoodie and lifted it up, exposing a sliver of light brown skin right above his belt. My cheeks heated even though the rest of my body was frozen, and I turned my head away.

The last thing in the world I needed was to look at his stomach, even if it was perfectly sculpted under the layers of baggy clothes.

He stuck the hoodie out to me with one hand while he tugged his shirt back down with the other but I shook my head. "I'm fine."

"You're stubborn. Take it before you freeze."

I would have rather frozen in place and forever be as still as the wax sculptures lining the walls beside us than accept his charity, but before I could react, he reached out and pulled me closer to him.

Gently, he placed the hoodie over my head, and I pulled my arms through the sleeves, taking note as my hands smoothed over soft fleece which was still warm from his body heat.

It smelled like him.

He spun me around to face him and checked me over once before meeting my eyes. The hint of a smile played at the corner of his mouth. "It looks good on you."

"Guys, look! That statue looks just like Avery." Someone shouted as everyone started to stare at me.

I'd been so distracted by Roland that I couldn't tell you a single figure we passed by. To be honest, I wasn't much of a history buff. Yeah, the Salem Witch Trials were horrible, but I didn't have much interest in learning each and every gruesome detail.

Roland, however, was all about it. It was all he could talk about for weeks leading up to today. Being forced to spend my afternoons with him for the past month had unexpectedly resulted in a history degree worth of lectures about Salem. He ran into the commotion while I stayed back.

"Holy smokes," he sa d, running back to me and grabbing my wrist to drag me up the hallway to what everyone was gawking at.

I looked into the case directly in front of where he stoppec. At first, all I could see was my own reflection. I took mental stock of the figure before me. Large violet eyes, bushy eyebrows, full lips with an over-pronounced cupid's bow. But as I looked closer, the image shifted. The long hair falling on either side of the pale shoulders was not dark brown like my own, but a sun-kissed blonde. The face staring back at me was a little older, a little smoother, a little more perfectly shaped. The wax statue and all of its similarity taunted me from its place inside the display.

The plaque below read, "Mary Kane, Execution by Hanging, September 22nd, 1692."

I stared, trying to convince myself it wasn't real. That this was some sort of horrible prank. There was no way to look at her without seeing myself. Her blonde hair and the colonial-era dress were the only indication that the glass case wasn't a mirror.

"Did you know you were a witch?" Roland asked, his voice interested but a little shaky.

"I'm not a witch, you idiot."

"Sure, looks like you."

Around her neck was a pendant- an exact replica of the one that hung from my neck. A purple stone encased in an intricate and graceful netting of golden knots and swirls. My own pendant grew hot where it lay against my chest and I slipped a hand between it and my bare skin, barely conscious of making the movement.

But it was enough to catch Roland's attention. He reached over and lifted the pendant, but I slapped his hand away and shot him a glare. His eyes pleaded with mine for an explanation, but I didn't have one to give him. Whispers made me turn and look, everyone pointing, judging. My classmates circled around me.

Even the adult chaperones looked cautious, wary. Suddenly the room became smaller. The temperature rose to a boiling point. Every eye was on me, sending arrows through my skin. As my classmates pointed at me and laughed, the adults whispered among themselves, too shocked to even register the vile things the kids were saying about me.

"I always knew she was weird," one voice said over the clamor of the others.

"Don't get too close. She'll put a spell on you." Another insulted from somewhere in the back.

The gasps, laughter, and jaunts were more than I could bear.

I ran.

I flew back through the halls of the museum, past the figures with their lifeless eyes boring holes into my soul. Emotions flooded my brain. I couldn't risk another incident like what happened at the school gym. I had to get away and process what I had just seen. I needed time, quiet, peace. There had to be someplace I could hide.

For so long I wanted to have a family, a history, like everyone else. But did I want a family if it meant inheriting one steeped in suspicion and scandal? Not just normal scandals, like that one uncle who drinks too much. No, it had to be one of the nation's biggest black marks in history. And the world today was still as cruel as it was during the Salem Witch Trials. Unsubstantiated information spread like wildfire. Mobs formed to terminate what they didn't understand or didn't agree with. So many times, the victims were harmless individuals. Like me.

The shame I felt when my classmates gawked at me was nothing I had ever experienced before and now I even felt shame for that shame. For being afraid to be different. For hoping that I wasn't connected to the woman the wax figure represented. And why? Because I didn't think that other people would accept it? Because I was worried about how it would make me look?

I was no better than the executioners. No better than the crooked judges and accusing priests. Scared of what was different. Scared to be seen as unique or strange. Scared of the unknown.

It was strange, this fear of the unknown. So much of my life was unknown. It was useless to be afraid of it now.

I didn't know who I truly was or even what my last name should have been... Avery Smith was just one of many abandoned and unwanted kids. A number in a file. Tracing my family history was impossible when I couldn't trace my own parents.

When I finally stopped running, I was at the memorial in the center of town. Face to face with *her* monument. I fell to my knees to read the inscription on the cement block. "MARY KANE HANGED SEPT 22, 1692"

Tears finally breached the fragile dam of my eyelids and fell against the ground. Tears I had held in for nearly sixteen years. Tears for a family I never had a chance to know. Tears for an alternate universe where I was loved, wanted. Tears for a possible ancestor that died for no reason. Tears that she may not be my ancestor. Tears for the realization that I was still completely alone.

A gentle hand rested on my shoulder. I slowed my breathing the best I could, wiped my eyes with the sleeve of Roland's hoodie, and prepared to tell a well-meaning stranger that I was alright. But when I looked up, it was Roland. Anger replaced my sadness. That little—how dare he follow me outside? Wasn't it obvious I wanted to be left alone? This boy was the last person I needed right now.

Before I could tell him so, thunder boomed above us. Lightning burst from the sky and struck the cement block in front of me. The bolt splintered midair and directed itself straight into the stone on my pendant. It burned hot against my skin. I looked down. A soft purple glow began to radiate from its center. Slowly my body lifted into the air and my arms fell backward, the pull like a string from my breastbone to some invisible point in the sky.

"Roland!" I screamed.

He reached for me, but I couldn't reach back. My arms wouldn't cooperate. They just hung like wet noodles despite how much effort I put in to moving them.

"Don't worry, Avery, I've got you!" He lunged toward me, trying to pull me back down.

I never felt his hands catch me.

Four

M y eyes opened to an overcast sky above me. Moisture seeped through my black jeans from the dew on the grass below me. A sickening feeling crept over my skin, as if I was being watched. I looked up to find Roland sitting right next to me, his knees drawn to his chest.

"Thank God you woke up," he said.

"Well, we see how helpful you are in an emergency. I'm literally struck by lightning and you can't even call the paramedics?" I was not surprised that he was a useless schmuck when crap actually hit the fan.

"Avery, look around. There are no paramedics to call. No hospitals. Barely any sign of civilization." He spread his arms out to indicate our surroundings.

I scoffed. We were in Salem, Massachusetts, not the Serengeti. Sure, it wasn't Boston, but it was still pretty civilized.

I turned my head. The monument was gone. The buildings had vanished. The creepy statues and stained-glass witches had disappeared.

In their wake was a flat field, lined by a dirt road with a line of trees on the other side. Off in the distance, I could make out small colonial style houses with smoke rising from their chimneys. I took in every detail, hoping to find clues to tell us where we could be. The sky was still dark, the same storm brewing from before we entered the wax museum. We couldn't have traveled too far.

"Where are we, Roland?" I asked.

"You tell me. You're the one with a witchy ancestor and a creepy necklace. If movies have taught me anything, you did whatever this is." I couldn't tell if he was joking.

Suddenly, I remembered my necklace. Had it broken in the lightning strike? My hand flew up, grasping for its familiar warm metal but it wasn't there. I flipped over to my hands and knees to search for it in case it had fallen off. The grass appeared to have grown eight inches in the last few minutes. I scoured the ground but found nothing.

"Don't be ridiculous. You don't actually buy that stuff, do you? Newsflash. Movies are fake." I was frustrated that my necklace was gone and had little patience for his insanity.

But the more I thought about it, he had a point. Had I done this? Well, not me, but maybe my bad luck was responsible. If so, it had really outdone itself this time. Burning curtains, exploding pipes, and inconvenient indoor rain were one thing. Relocating both myself and Roland to an unknown place? That was going a bit far.

If Mary Kane was my ancestor, she was probably cursed with bad luck too. That's why she was tried as a witch and ended up in the gallows. If destruction followed her around as it followed me, people could easily confuse it as some evil power.

I stood up to dust myself off but suddenly felt dizzy and sat back down. Roland looked at me, appearing concerned. He took my chin between his fingers and turned my head from side to side.

"You don't look like you've been struck by lightning," he said as if people who were struck by lightning turned green or had some other visible marker.

"Do you know what that would even look like?"

Roland got lost in his monologue about the effects of lightning on the human body like he was a doctor. I think he just liked hearing himself sound smart because he had to have known I wasn't listening.

He took my wrist in his hand, pressing down with two fingers. My skin burned where it met his. My cheeks grew warm. I didn't care for human touch. Every once in a while, a well-meaning foster mom thought hugs could "fix" me. That never lasted long and touch became an unwelcome reminder that whatever was wrong with me couldn't be healed by hugs, or anything else for that matter.

I yanked my hand back and shot him a look that could wilt flowers.

He held up his hands in surrender.

"Just checking your pulse to make sure everything's running right on the inside."

I slowly and cautiously gave him my hand. As much as I couldn't stand being touched, I needed to know how badly the lightning strike had affected me.

Matching my cautious movements, he closed his hand over mine. I shut my eyes tightly and tried to imagine I was anywhere but here with Roland.

After a moment, his hands left my wrist and I felt his fingers grasp my chin lightly and tilt it upwards.

"Okay Avery, you've got to look at me now."

I opened my eyes slowly and found him staring back at me through the lenses of his glasses. His eyes were definitely hazel. Not brown, not green, but a mix of the two. The tiny sunbursts near his pupils reminded me of wild sunflowers.

My mind drifted back to when I was seven. A drive in the backseat of a caseworker's car from one failed foster home to another. A field of sunflowers for as far as the eye could see. I had begged to stop and look at them. To touch one, though what I really wanted to do was run with abandon through them. But we were on a schedule and caseworkers have no time for small girls who love flowers.

"Can you follow my finger?" Roland's question broke my reverie. He held up his index finger and slowly moved it from side to side. I followed it as instructed.

"Not with your head. Keep it straight like you're looking at me and just use your eyes."

I obeyed. His caramel-colored skin was perfect. I was a bit jealous of his tiny pores and oil-free forehead. I was willing to bet the boy didn't even own any zit cream.

The golden hues of his skin were natural, genetic beauty. His complexion a perfect mix of shades that seemed to catch the sunlight, making him nearly glow like the golden boy everyone thought he was.

Following his finger with my eyes was more difficult than I thought it would be. With his face so close to mine, I couldn't think of anything else than how beautiful he was. I hated myself. The last thing I needed was to fall for Roland and set myself up for another heartbreak. Love was stupid but it was even worse when it was with someone who barely knew you existed, except to annoy you or benefit off you.

"Yep, you're good," he said as he swiftly pulled his hand away and set about rifling through his backpack that had somehow managed to survive our trip.

"Jerky?" he asked as he poked me in the cheek with a greasy brown stick.

I swatted it away and glowered. Even amazing skin couldn't make up for his annoying personality.

A clunking noise came from down the dirt road, and we turned to see a freaking horse and wagon. I would have assumed we had been transported to an Amish community if it weren't for the people driving. With their waistcoats and funky hats, they were unquestionably not Amish. They looked more like the figures in the wax museum.

"Run!" Roland half yelled, half whispered.

"What?"

He grabbed my arm and pulled me along with him, hiding behind a boulder. Catching our breath, we contorted our bodies so we would both fit behind the large stone. I could smell his cologne, or was it his shampoo? Either way, it smelled like the suburbs after a fresh snow. Like icicles melting off the gutters of steeped roofs and the burning embers in a fireplace.

"I may not know what's going on but one thing is for sure, we cannot be seen. At least until we get a grip on our surroundings," Roland whispered.

"And what do you think has happened? Because my best guess is we got knocked unconscious and someone is playing a prank on us. This is probably one of those reenactments. They have those here, you know."

Roland looked at me dubiously. I glanced away. Even I knew the whole thing could not be explained by conventional logic. People don't just get struck by lightning with no effects. They don't find wax statues of witches that look just like them. And they sure as hell don't wake up to colonial villagers driving horse-drawn wagons.

The horses stopped their trot on the dirt road, the carriage stilled, and the passengers disembarked, fanning out, searching.

"Are they looking for us?" I asked quietly.

"Probably. They would have seen the lightning strike from that village over there." His eyes scanned the horizon. "There's nowhere else to hide. We're going to have to make a break for it to the trees on the other side of the road."

"Okay, on my mark," I said. He could think he had our situation figured out, but I had him beat in the running department. I had been running every moment of my life. I was prepared for this. I ran better than I did anything else, whether it was away from my problems or away from painful memories.

"Avery, wait. Listen, if they catch me, keep running. It doesn't do any good for the both of us to get caught."

I gave him a doubtful stare. "You big baby."

The men closed in. Their voices floated up to us and their heavy footsteps grew closer.

"Go," I said, leaping from my crouch and dashing toward the trees.

Roland kept pace with me. I was nearly there when a man stepped in front of me. Momentum kept me hurtling toward him even as I tried to correct my course.

He grabbed me around the waist, sending us both to the ground. I landed on my ankle, and there was a sickening crunch. Pain raced through me like a thousand knives piercing through my flesh. It was full seconds before I realized the scream sounding in my ears was my own. And then everything went black.

When I came to, my hands and ankles were tied together. The ropes seared like fire where they touched my skin, especially my injured leg. The men shouted. It had to be English, but I didn't understand everything they were saying. Roland had either escaped or was being held somewhere else.

My throat burned as I cried out for him. The men shoved a cloth in my mouth to muffle the sound and when I didn't think things could get worse, the sky rumbled, opened up, and it started pouring.

The men didn't flinch from the rain, and they made no effort to guard themselves against the downpour, nor did they offer me any cover. Picking me up like a sack of potatoes, they threw me into the back of the wagon. They poked and prodded at my clothes until they found my phone in my pocket.

"What sort of bewitched device is this?" one of them hissed.

I tried to answer but couldn't with the cloth filling my mouth.

There was more shouting and yelling, along with some barely legible grunts, from the mob.

"Why have you risen from hell to torment these lands?" a man growled.

I said nothing. I was starting to understand the gravity of the situation and it was obvious whatever mess my bad luck had thrown me into wasn't going to be solved with another foster family or another move. I was royally screwed this time. And with Roland as my only hope, I could go ahead and count on figuring this out on my own.

After painfully bouncing around in the carriage for what felt like forever, we finally stopped outside of a grey rock and mortar building with numerous heavy wooden doors dotting the side I could see at intervals. I lifted myself to stare out of the side of the wagon as a man slid a thin black key into one of the iron locks and the door opened to reveal nothing but darkness.

"Keep her with the other vile witch until she can be rightly questioned," a commanding voice boomed.

Chapter Three

A minuscule amount of light filtered through the cracks in the mortar, barely enough to make out my own hands in front of me. I laid down on the cold damp mix of dirt and straw beneath me. The smell of stale bread and human excrement made me wretch.

"By heavens, have they not yet finished with their ridiculous crusade?" a quiet, strained voice said from the other side of the room.

A girl about my age leaned forward into one of the thin beams of light. Her dark hair was matted and she wore a tattered, simple dress that was stained with dirt and grime.

She lifted her head and lavender eyes gazed at me from under thick lashes, just like the wax statue's. Only with darker hair.

"Mary Kane?" I tried; highly doubtful it was her but caught up in the strangeness of everything that had happened.

"No, Mary is—" she stopped herself. A wave of sadness radiated from her. "My apologies. Mary was my sister. She has now escaped this world and its ignorant people. I am Anne Kane."

She made her way over to me. I scooted away, slamming hard into the rock wall behind me.

Kneeling, she brought her face to my level and pushed a lock of black curls away from my eyes. Then it was her turn to back away startled. She sunk to her knees and her head fell forward.

"Where did they find you, my darling kin? How did you come to this place of hatred and judgment?"

I had nothing to lose by telling this woman the truth. My best chance of survival was to be honest and hope someone else knew what was going on. She sat patiently as I recounted every detail from the moment Roland, and I arrived at the wax museum. She never once looked at me with judgment or skepticism. She took every word as truth.

When I finished my story, I looked up from where I'd been starting at the ground to find tears sliding down her cheeks.

"You've come all this way, but yet you find yourself in the one place where your fate is doomed. They took my sister to the gallows only yesterday. They will soon take us both as well."

"How though? How have I come all this way?"

"Do you not realize the power you possess within? Did you not call upon the heavens for the lightning bolt which brought you here?"

"What are you talking about? I didn't ask to be struck by lightning. I don't have powers. No one has powers. That's all just folklore and superstition to explain what science can't." Even if I was temporarily rendered insane by the lightning, or having some sort of horrid nightmare, it was no excuse to buy into her delusions.

I tried to move away and promptly fell when a sharp pain stabbed up my leg. I caught myself on an uneven stone protruding from the wall.

"Are you hurt?" Anne asked in a kind tone.

I sent a sidelong glance in her direction. "It's a broken ankle, I think. Happened when they tackled me."

"Come now. I can repair that which ails you."

I sighed and relented. I was trapped in a room no larger than a standard walk-in closet with this woman. What was the point of fighting?

She gathered some straw from the floor and reached up to my hair again. I closed my eyes and braced myself for the affection.

There was a shock of pain at the top of my head and my eyes flew open.

"What the hell did you just do?"

"I apologize if that was uncomfortable. I must have a few strands of your hair for this to work."

I watched suspiciously as she formed the straw and hair into a doll. Memories of documentaries on the history channel told me this was a poppet. Something like the equivalent of a voodoo doll.

She pulled a pin from the seam of her dress.

"Wait!" I yelled as she stuck the pin into the doll.

The pain in my ankle immediately dissipated. I rotated my foot back and forth in disbelief.

She held up the doll. The sharp end of the pin protruded from the bottom of the doll's makeshift leg.

I slid one hand over my face and tightly closed my eyes.

Taking a deep breath, I allowed myself to finally say the one word I had been avoiding.

"So, we *are* witches?"

"We have been called many names. Witch, sorceress, the damned, the wicked. But know this, we are the blessed. The earth and the heavens have chosen us as their vessels and allowed us to harness their power."

"We must have two different kinds of magic then because I'm pretty sure I'm just cursed." My throat tightened and tears threatened to spill. I was too strong to cry over this. All those tears had dried up long ago.

"Oh, my darling. Did your female kin do not teach you how to harness your darkness?"

"I don't have a family. Never have. I guess they knew how much trouble I would be." I had resigned myself to this fact over the years. It was as much a part of me as the curse was. I'd known for as long as I could remember that my family abandoned me. That I was too much for even my own parents to take. That they knew how much trouble I'd be and escaped while they could. I couldn't blame them. I didn't want to be part of my life either.

"Your family is standing in front of you now. Yet surely, your counterbalance is back in your time. It's a wonder you have survived this long without her."

She reached over to take my hand.

"How strong must you be, to handle all the darkness, chaos, and destruction of your blessing without the light, order, and creation of your sister's to balance you. It has only been a day and I can already feel the darkness wearing at my soul."

"Mary was your light," I said, hearing the grief in her voice.

"And my twin. My sister. My other half. The best of the two of us." Her eyes fixed on the ground. "Now I fear I'm too weakened to save myself from the same fate."

A noise at the side of the building caught our attention as one of the rocks in the wall slid loose. The burst of light from the gap temporarily blinded me. I scrambled away from the light and into the back corner like a cockroach on the kitchen floor. Anne ran toward it.

"Ezra?" she whispered into the opening.

"I come bearing bread this evening, Anne." It was a boy's voice. A package wrapped in cloth slid into the space.

"You are so wonderful to me in my last days, sweet Ezra."

"Tis the least I can do to make up for the wickedness of the town and its people's hysterical ways."

Anne laid down flat on the ground to talk through the hole to the boy on the other side. She told him about my arrival and the strange way I got here. She turned her attention to me when she was done.

"Ezra is an orphan from the village. My mother gave him charity several years ago before her death. He has been bringing me food and water so I can survive this evil place."

"Do you think he could find Roland? He's not worth much, but it's possible he could find a way to help get us out of here."

"You brought someone with you?" the voice outside the wall asked.

"Yes, a boy. Almost sixteen. He's got tight brown curls that fall in his face and he wears glasses."

"Glasses?" The boy's confusion was evident.

"Umm." I grappled to remember the word used for glasses in this century. "Spectacles. Also, he's wearing strange clothes for your time."

The boy laughed. "I do not think he will still be in those. Goody Catherine from up the road caused quite the stir a little while ago. It seems someone stole the clothes drying on her line."

Roland was more cunning than I gave him credit for. A flicker of hope spread through me knowing he was alive and safe, not that I would ever admit that to him. If I ever saw him again.

"If I were to find him, what help could we give? I have toiled for weeks trying to find a way to help the Kane sisters. It shall be my life's regret that I was unable to save Mary," Ezra said.

Anne whipped her head up and looked at me. "Your amplifier. Was the crystal within damaged by the lightning? Did they remove it from you when you were brought here?" she asked, gears clearly moving in her mind.

"Amplifier?"

"Your necklace, amulet, charm. Different sisters wear it different ways. It's meant to amplify your power. There are only two in existence and it has been passed down to each new generation."

I put my hand against the bare spot on my chest where my necklace usually sat. So, it wasn't just a useless piece of costume jewelry after all. "I lost it somehow. It wasn't around my neck when I woke up here. I looked for it but couldn't find it."

She paused and seemed to think twice about her question. "No, I would think not," she said somberly. "One object cannot exist twice within the same time. Even our powers cannot change such a simple law."

One object? Twice in the same time? My amulet must have been passed down from Anne herself.

"Where is yours then?" I asked.

"It is being stored as evidence against me. It was nearly the only non-spectral evidence they had until you arrived."

I was confused. "Non-spectral?"

"It's the only evidence they have that is solid. The rest is mere testimony and words."

"It's in old Sherriff Corwin's house," Ezra said, clearly glad to have something to add to the conversation. "That is where they keep everything. I saw them take the black square they got from Avery in there. It's the talk of the town. Or at least it was until the clothes went missing."

Just then someone called Ezra's name, the voice sounding loud and angry. The light disappeared as he hastily shoved the rock back into place. Raised voices and scuffling were muffled through the walls but I could clearly hear Ezra pleading for forgiveness.

"What will happen to him if they find out he's helping us?"

"Ezra is a smart boy. He keeps himself out of trouble. But his life is uncharmed, to say the least. The preacher that took him in as a babe is a godly man but not a kind one. That's why Mother took care of him as much as she could. We made sure he knew that not all people are as horrible as the preacher."

"So that was the preacher calling for him?"

"Aye, it must be nearing dusk now. Ezra will need to bring in his keep for the day and do his duties."

"His keep?"

"He is to pay his own way in this world. Begging, stealing, bartering. However, he can make money for his guardian.

Has been this way since he was old enough to toddle. Will be this way until he can leave."

"Do you think he and Roland can actually help us?" I asked, afraid of the potentially misplaced hope that still lingered in my chest.

"If they manage to get the amulet to us, then I can teach you how to harness it and use the crystal within. I would do it myself, but I have relied on my counterweight so long I am not sure I would be able to contain and control the darkness it will require."

"How long do you think we have?"

"I have already been sentenced as a witch. My execution will not be long now. That is, if I make it until then. I fear I do not have many more sunrises left within me."

Five

A nne was more correct than she realized. The next morning the men that captured me opened the door to throw in bits of stale bread and some sort of stew. The liquid splattered on the dirt floor and turned it into mud. Anne crawled over to the door and began to pick what little meat she could find up off the floor. If this was what Anne was surviving off, it was no surprise that her health was failing.

"Eat up, you vile woman. This meal shall be your last. By tomorrow's daybreak, your neck will be in a noose," one of the men spat at Anne as he kicked her away from the door. His leather boot connected with her rib cage, and she gasped for air.

We had to get out of here and now we were racing against the clock. I hoped Ezra had found Roland. It was our only chance of survival. Relying on others was hard enough for me when my life wasn't in danger. Now it was absolute torture. Roland was smart, but still, I had to hope that it was enough.

While we waited, feeling impudent for our inability to change our own fate, Anne taught me as much of my power as she could without my amulet or my counterbalance.

Apparently, the crystal within had been brought from our homeland, somewhere in Europe. It recognized the energy behind our feelings, the natural wavelengths that were given off by our bodies.

"You must channel your emotions," she began. "Look deep within your heart to find the seeds of your actions. I can see the chaos in your eyes. It is clear that you possess the night. Fire, lightning, darkness, chaos, destruction. They are all at your command as long as you respect their power."

"Why would anyone want to harness destruction unless they were evil? Why can't I just use a wand to unlock doors or something? You know, say some Latin words and flick a stick. Then bam, done."

She looked at me, her expression showing she was confused and exasperated. "Magic does not work that way. You may be a vessel with the blessed ability to wield such power, but it is not yours alone. A soldier may use the sword to cut, but he himself cannot slice."

After gathering a small mound of dirt from the floor and picking it up, she closed her eyes. A small flicker of a flame shaped itself in the center of her palm and quickly extinguished. She slid back against the wall, clearly exhausted.

"See? You ask the earth for its power and use it accordingly. I am in no condition to display the mighty ways you may manipulate the elements to your will. The months within this confinement, fighting rats for my food and living in my own filth, combined with the grief from Mary's passing, has made me too weak. But Mary and I were once an impressive sight."

Her eyes closed and a smile flickered across her face as she leaned over to touch her fingertips lightly to my temple.

The dark cell faded and a blonde woman, the inverse coloration of Anne but otherwise so much like her, appeared laughing in my mind. She twirled in a cotton dress surrounded by a field of flowers before she looked over playfully at me, the pendant around her neck glowing softly. The flowers began to grow and twist, creating a canopy above her.

"Come play, Annie," she called out to me, and I looked down to find I was dressed in similar clothing. I moved forward without consciously moving my feet.

"Don't play with your powers out here, Mary. Grandmother said it could be dangerous now," I said, as Anne's voice escaped my lips.

"We're alone. No one will see us. Now give us some rain to dance in, sister," Mary said.

Something grew in my chest, making it difficult to breathe for a few heartbeats until I waved my hand and the sky clouded. Rain started to fall, light and warm. Mary danced around, her hands motioning in different directions as she bent the sunbeams to create a cascade of rainbows that surrounded us. She giggled and fell backward, a net of vines catching her mid-air. She beckoned to me to come lay with her and I did. We stared at the sky as I shaped the clouds into objects to entertain her.

Just as we heard voices coming through the woods, the image dissipated, and I came back to reality. Anne had completely collapsed on the ground and her breathing was labored.

"Rest. I require rest," she managed to say before she closed her eyes and drifted off.

I sat in the dark cell and tried to come to terms with all of the revelations. Everything I knew about myself, and my past had changed. I still didn't know why my parents abandoned me, or if what Anne said about my having a sister was true, but I knew I once had a family that could have loved me even if it was gone now. That was a more startling revelation than the fact that I could do magic.

After what felt like hours alone in the darkness, I decided to recreate Anne's fire trick. I closed my eyes and focused on my emotions. I wasn't sure how to show respect to the elements like Anne directed but whispered the dirt a thank you just in case that worked. It didn't.

I heard Anne stirring behind me.

"You aren't being honest with yourself, Avery," she said, her voice weak and raspy. "Close your eyes again. Now, think of this: when a tree dies, its decay feeds the new saplings underneath it." She took a break to breathe deeply. "In this way, chaos and destruction are needed to create growth and order. You cannot hate the dark and wield it at the same time. You must embrace the dark parts of yourself. Let yourself feel what you avoid so vehemently."

I held the dirt again in my palm and attempted to dig deep to find things that I didn't want to think about. I pulled on the memory of the unfortunate gym incident at my last school. The smack of the basketball against the back of my head. The jaunts of the other girls behind me. The crack of thunder that echoed inside the building from wall to wall. The burnt smel. of the backboard on the basketball hoop where the lightning scorched it. The screams of my classmates as they slippec and slid across the slick floor as they scrambled to get out.

I felt the same heaviness in my chest and imagined myself channeling it into the dirt in my hand. Bursts of light exploded and my eyes flew open. Tiny sparks dotted the ceiling like stars and then flickered out almost immediately.

"Good," Anne said. "You are making progress. You should be able feel it in your blood, the forces at play. Now you must work harder to harness them. This would be easier to teach you if we were back at our—" she interrupted herself with a weak coughing fit, "—my home with Mary's herbs and my spells."

I practiced as much as possible. I was hoping I could learn to master my little flickers of flame and perhaps burn the door open. If it worked and we moved fast enough, I might have time to get Anne into the woods before anyone came to put out the fire.

No matter how hard I focused, how deep I dug into my memories, I couldn't get the tiny embers to come together and form one small flame. I felt hopeless. Even with our supernatural powers, there was no chance for escape. Between Anne being too weak to perform any magic, and me not being able to control my own, we might as well be sitting ducks.

Anne watched me intently until we heard shouts coming from outside of the wall, a cacophony of voices sounding all at once. Anne struggled to dislodge the stone Ezra had moved earlier but was too weak to force it from its place. I went over and pulled it loose. Through the gap, I could see boots running through the mud, slinging it in all directions. I moved slightly to let Anne see.

"That's the direction of the Corwin house," she said after a moment.

"Do you think that means that Roland and Ezra were able to get the amulet?"

"We will have to wait and see. There is no way to know if they were successful or if the mob is to apprehend them. Those men have nothing but wickedness and fear in their hearts," she said as she replaced the stone.

Only moments later, the loose stone flew into our dark prison, spraying dirt in the air as it ricocheted off the ground. Something came in directly behind it and glimmered in the beam of light. The sounds of footfalls running in the opposite direction echoed inside, followed by another round of shouting men and heavy boots racing by.

Anne scrambled to the object and held it in her hands. I had never seen someone look at a material possession with such love. She pressed her lips to the gold circle and then slid it around her neck. Her body began to radiate, her veins filling with a glowing wine-colored liquid. The violet of her eyes shone bright in the darkness, two lilac blooms against the darkness around us.

SIX

T he lock on the outside of the door shook violently against its handle until the wood splintered and then disintegrated into what looked like rotten mulch. The bright sunlight exploded into the room and stung my eyes. Anne tried to run but gaining her magic had done nothing for her physical strength and she collapsed.

I threw her arm over my neck and carried her out. My own body wasn't entirely up to the challenge, but I pressed on. Once outside, I could see a crowd of men running toward the center of town, chasing two women, or what looked to be women.

Roland's voice was surprisingly sweet to my ears as I heard him call out behind him to the men.

"Faster, you lubbers, you won't bring home supper tonight with that pace!"

I could recognize it even under the feminine lilt he tried to imitate. The dresses and bonnets Roland and Ezra wore were ill-fitting on the two teenage boys as elbows and knees escaped the bonds of the cloth as they ran. The men held torches, pitchforks, and shovels as they chased them through the village's dirt streets.

With the men distracted, I was able to get Anne deep enough into the woods that anyone who came to check out the now decayed door of our cell would not be able to see us.

"Where do we go from here?" I asked her when I was confident that we were far enough away from the men.

"We need to get to my cottage. There are supplies and knowledge there that can help you, and things I cannot leave town without. Our history will be lost if I am unable to save them."

"Anne, the history *was* lost. I am all that is left of the Kanes. The only thing that has survived is this pendant." I rested my hand against the crystal encircled inside the gold and a wave of energy washed over me. Anne's chest lifted as if the pendant was pulling her toward me and she smiled.

"The crystal recognizes you now. It feels your power."

I reached out my hand again and a string of light left the necklace and floated softly to my fingertips. I tingled where it met my skin and I jumped back.

"You are too scared of your power to wield it properly. There is a limit to the amount of magic we can do without being consumed by the darkness, but you will not find it is easy to do. You do not have to be afraid of that."

"Wait, what? What do you mean we can be consumed by the darkness? You didn't warn me that was a possibility," I nearly yelled before I remembered that we were hiding.

"Do not be afraid. As I said, it takes quite a bit of energy at once to be in danger. Your soul will let you know when you are close to your limit. It cannot be done on accident," she said as she started slowly walking further into the wooded area.

Since I didn't have much of a choice, I followed her. Her every movement was labored with exhaustion.

"Can't we, like, fly?" I asked after the first mile or so of walking while she leaned on me.

"Fly? Like a bird?" she said, not even looking at me.

"Yeah, like on a broom or something?"

"If I were stronger, it is possible I could use the wind to elevate you and propel you forward, but it would feel more like a stone being skipped than a bird soaring."

I imagined myself bobbing up and down across the forest floor and decided it was probably better for my health if we didn't try.

"Regardless, we are nearly there," she continued.

After a few hundred feet we came upon a clearing. The dimness of the forest gave way to a sunny field full of flowers and herbs. A waft of lavender and basil filled my sinuses and I sneezed, though the smell was pleasant.

"That would be Mary's work," Anne said. "Plants adored her and she them. Your own sister will share the same gift. It is the light's way."

Beyond the field, a small cabin sat tucked against a rock outcropping. Alongside it, a stream bubbled past quietly. Ivy covered the homes outside walls and tall flowers seemed to look in the windows.

Inside, the house seemed to be one large room. A stone fireplace took up most of the back while three beds lined the walls. Herbs hung from the ceiling; books littered the tables and crystals of various colors were scattered throughout. Vials of glowing liquid and jars of animal bones were neatly arranged on shelves.

Anne took her time opening drawers and looking underneath books.

"Where did she put it?" she exclaimed after looking in the hundredth place.

"Put what? What are you looking for?"

She didn't answer. Finally, she suddenly stopped and looked up at me.

"Of course," she said under her breath as she ran back outside, leaving me in the house by myself.

I could hear her talking to someone and poked my head out the door. She stood in front of one of the largest flowers, seemingly conversing with it. She lifted her hand and grazed one of the petals and the bloom tilted down toward her. A glimmer of gold slid down its long stem and directly into her outstretched hand.

She thanked it by taking a pile of leaves, decomposing them into near dust, and placing them near the flower's roots. It was fertilizer, I realized.

As she walked back into the house I asked, "If all of this is here, why do your accusers only have spectral evidence? Why haven't they raided this place?"

"A man without the blessing would only see trees here. He may smell the lavender or hear those that dwell within, but he cannot see nor feel what you can. Not without the permission of a blessed sister," she answered.

"So, if you stayed here and never left, you would be safe."

"Safe but alone. My grandmother has been taken by illness and my sister by men. What is a life that isn't shared but is the mere passing of time?" she replied stoically.

"Being alone isn't that bad," I said, turning so she couldn't see my face. "I've been alone my entire life. You get used to it."

Her hand rested on my back and the tingle of the amulet's tentacle-like light caressed my shoulder.

"You've never been truly alone. We were always there," she said. I turned to face her, my eyebrows knitted together in confusion, and the chain of the necklace started to rise on its own until it hovered over my head and dropped into place around my neck. Its warm glow enveloped me.

"We?"

"Every Kane woman has carried either this crystal or its mate. A piece of each of their souls lies within, guiding you along your way."

I thought back to every time I thought I had misplaced the necklace and found it somewhere too obvious, each time I had moved and not a soul dared to take it even though all my other earthly possessions had been lost. Even that morning on the bus when my necklace had smacked Roland on the head, giving me the advantage, I needed to get my phone back from him. Maybe it was true that the crystal helped guide me.

Outside the small window on the front of the house, we saw the boys come across the clearing, stripping off women's clothing as they approached. Now that I could see Ezra clearly, he looked strangely familiar. Blonde curls bounced above wide shoulders as he made his way through the field, and his lips were thin with an ever-present smirk. He was thin, too thin, perhaps because of his unfortunate circumstances, but tall.

He had clearly been given authority to see the cabin as he walked with purpose toward us, carefully avoiding the rows of planted herbs and flowers. Roland, on the other hand, stumbled his way through, pushing aside invisible branches and stepping over fallen logs that weren't there. I shouldn't have been as amused as I was. He looked so serious, concentrating so hard on making his way through the imaginary brush like a man on a mission. It took everything I had not to bust out laughing at the sight.

"Oh dear," Anne said as she held her hand out for the amulet. I lifted it off my neck with some reluctance. Now that I knew what it was capable of, I never wanted to be without it again.

She mumbled something in another language under her breath and Roland's head shot up from where he was intently focused on the forest floor in front of him.

"Woah," was his only response to the field and cabin that must have seemed to appear from thin air.

"So, there *are* Latin words then?" I asked Anne, excited that this might be the magic I knew from television and movies.

"Charms and hexes require spells. If you need to alter something involving another human, you must ask for help with more than just your soul."

Ezra cleared his throat, causing us to turn and look at him. He took one of my hands as he bowed on one knee in front of me. He lifted my hand to his mouth and placed a gentle kiss just below my wrist, his lips lingering a little too long for my comfort.

"I have not yet had the pleasure to formally meet you," he said as he raised his head back up. "I must say, you are quite beautiful, Avery."

Anne swatted at him with the skirts of her dress.

"You libertine. You honestly believe yourself to be a philanderer, do you?" she shouted as she chased him, however feebly, back out into the field.

"That was weird," Roland said as he came to stand beside me.

"I assure you that is one of the least weird things I have seen today," I responded.

Anne was too tired from the trek home and all that had happened to chase Ezra far. Satisfied that she made her point, she returned to our sides at the front of the cabin.

Moments later, we heard voices echo through the woods and dogs barking.

"Were you followed?" she asked the boys.

"I do not think so. And if we were, they would not find us beyond the trees. You know this," Ezra answered.

She lowered her voice to a hushed whisper.

"We must all go inside the house. They may not be able to see us, but let us not give them any reason to look. Lest you forget Ezra, they took Mary from this place."

"Yes, but she allowed herself to be seen. She surrendered," Ezra replied.

"Only so they would not take me. Her sacrifice will not be in vain. I have a responsibility to live now," she said, looking pointedly in my direction.

seven

The four of us crouched as low as we could inside the cabin as the voices became louder. We all stared out of the tiny window as hunting dogs appeared at the tree line and sniffed in our direction.

"Can you sedate them as Mary could?" Ezra asked Anne.

"Animals are within the realm of light. Nothing I do will be as strong as Mary's natural tendency to the light."

She closed her eyes and the amulet lit up again. The dogs halted for a moment, shook their heads, and then appeared to become even more determined to sniff us out.

"I don't think that's what he had in mind," Roland said.

She shot him a glare that could cut stone. "If you believe you could control those beasts better than I, please do. It would be lovely to know we are in the presence of another witch."

Roland looked thoroughly chastised as he stared at the floor.

The men closed in on the cabin, unable to see the clearing they stood in, making their way through what they thought was a dense forest.

"Halt! This is where we apprehended the sister. The same strange smell lingers here," one of the men called out.

"There is nothing here but trees and underbrush," another replied.

"Nonetheless, bring me the torches. We will smoke out the thieves and the escaped witches at once."

"No. No. No," Anne repeated, shaking her head and grabbing the sides of it. "The veil does not work against elements. Only living beings."

"Can we stop the fire? Make it rain like you showed me in that memory?"

"My powers are too weak. I cannot do it alone with Mary gone."

I looked down at my own hands. I hadn't been able to consolidate embers into a larger flame, much less manipulate the clouds and rain. I didn't have an amulet to help me. But I felt the pull in my chest, my emotions rising to the surface. Now that I had a relative, I wasn't going to lose her.

"You aren't alone," I said as I held out my hand and tiny sparks of lightning flew in between my fingertips, surprising even me. "There are two Kane witches in this cabin."

"I knew you were a witch!" Roland exclaimed, and the men quickly looked in our direction, alerted by his outburst.

"Seriously, Roland. You can gloat later. Right now, let's try not to die, okay?" I said behind clenched teeth.

He shrugged but quieted down. "Makes more sense about the Ficus trees, though."

Anne grabbed several jagged crystals of varying hues of blue and a small wooden bowl as the men outside began to set fire all around the cabin.

"Mary's amulet is attuned to the light so It will not amplify your powers as your own would," she said as she placed the crystals in a circle. "We will need more than just a little rain. This should help."

We sat opposite of each other, the boys watching as she put her hand in mine and began to chant.

"Clouds of black, clouds of white. Come to me and show thy might. Bring us rain, beneath your water, extinguish the flame."

I closed my eyes and let my fear and anger bubble to the surface. I felt a tug deep inside of me, as if my very soul was attempting to pull loose.

"Look deeper. Find something darker. Allow yourself to feel hurt and anger as you never have before," she commanded over the growing sounds of thunder.

I could feel the heat. The fires must have been burning closer to the cabin.

I tried to pull on painful memories. All the moving. All the rejections and lost families. Every time I hoped for a permanent home and lost it.

Lightning surged and the light penetrated my eyelids, making dancing patterns across my vision, but there was no sound of rain.

Someone grabbed my chin and I looked up to find Roland holding my face close to his.

He leaned in and brought his lips to mine, locking me in a kiss. The thunder stopped and the clouds started to dissipate as I reveled in his honey taste.

"Boy, what have you done?" Anne yelled.

"It was supposed to piss her off. Make her angry enough to bring the rain," Roland replied, his eyes never leaving mine.

"You are clearly not as bright as you think you are if you thought that would work," Ezra said with a chuckle.

Stunned, I said nothing.

"We're running out of time, we must try again," Anne said as I heard the hiss and crackle of the flames.

We closed our eyes, and she continued her chant from earlier.

"Release thy lightning and set free thy thunder, bring us now a storm down under."

I thought about the kiss, of Roland. Of getting us out of this mess. I thought of him surrounded by flames, caught in the middle of my latest bout of bad luck.

Thunder sounded again and the sweet patter of rain began.

Since it was working, I dug deeper. I thought of this being my fault. Of dragging him into this. Of Roland dying like a 17th century peasant just because I happened to wander into his life. I felt a storm forming inside my chest. Black clouds circled my lungs, my heartbeat boomed like thunder.

The rain fell harder, massive drops making their way through the roof and onto my face.

The fire popped and sizzled as it started to go out and the smell of smoke filled my lungs. Coughing and sputtering, we made our way out of the cabin, seeking refuge from the dense air left behind by the death of the flames.

Ezra had to carry Anne, as the experience left her even more weakened than before, but she managed to gather the remaining sparks with her magic and move them to the nearby stream.

Ezra laid Anne down beside the water bank as Roland and I walked the perimeter to make sure we were really alone. The men appeared to have taken shelter from the storm in the forest. All that was left was the singed earth that was recently a bountiful field.

"We must get you home before they come back for me," Anne said weakly.

"I'm not even sure how I got here. I have no idea how to get back," I responded.

"Time manipulation is not a traditional skill of the blessed. It takes too much darkness, too much power and it's possible to damage the crystal beyond repair or for the witch be consumed. But you cannot stay here so I must try. You belong in your own time. Here you are in too much danger."

Ezra pulled her to face him. His face was tight with worry.

"I cannot allow you to do this, Anne. I fear I could not survive if I lost you."

"Oh, sweet Ezra. It is lose me this way or lose me to those men. Would you rather I be strung up for the world to watch? This way at least there is a chance that the blessing will live on."

"Wait, what happens if you're consumed?" I asked, that word hitting me like a ton of bricks. "Does that mean I would cease to exist?"

"A consumed soul does not die. Should I succumb to the darkness, I will never feel the light again, but I will live on. Preserved in perfect darkness for as long as my mortal body can sustain. I will never again know happiness or joy."

"I can't let you do that," I said.

"We have no other choice."

She closed her eyes and the amulet lit up with the glowing tendrils that meant she was drawing on its strength.

"No!" I yelled as the sky began to darken again.

As thunder clapped overhead, a massive snarling dog appeared behind Ezra, leaping on him and pinning him to the ground.

Anne stopped trying to use her magic to send me home and started toward the dog, mumbling spells under her breath. The look of determination and anger hardened her features and the exhausted limp disappeared from her step.

Nothing made the beast relinquish his hold until two men ran up and grabbed Ezra from under the dogs pinning him on the ground.

"Run!" Ezra yelled; his voice muffled by the arms ensnaring him. But Anne didn't move. Her violet eyes grew to dark purple pools and the amulet vibrated violently against her chest.

Black streams of energy, like the darkest ink, shot from her hands and into the men's chests. They collapsed on the ground, their bodies turning to ash as they fell.

Ezra looked down at the men's remains, his expression one of confusion.

"Did—did you murder them?" he managed to sputter out after a moment.

"They would have murdered us," Anne replied, nearly in tears. "Do not think me evil." The tears then began to fall. "I must protect my family, the ones I love," she sobbed.

"Anne, we have to leave this place. Travel far from here and never look back," Ezra said.

"I know," Anne replied as she let herself collapse against him. "I know."

She slid to the ground, his grip slowing her. Her eyes closed and her body went limp.

"No!" I yelled, running toward them.

"Is she breathing?" Roland asked, his face concerned as he appeared right beside me.

I placed my hand under her nose.

Luckily, a light and gentle breath passed over my fingers. She was still alive, but barely.

EIGHT

I got up and ran into the cabin, searching Anne's notes for any sort of healing potion. The writing was almost too elaborate for me to read. Calligraphy sprawled over what felt like thousands of pages. Potions for colds and broken bones, spells for love. Roland ran in behind me and the hair on the back of my neck stood on end due to his presence. Even a life-or-death situation didn't seem to distract my body from the thought of our kiss.

I set him to work immediately to distract myself and keep on task.

"Look through the pages and find anything for healing!" I yelled to him.

Roland did as he was instructed, searching through the pages of parchment, matching my rapid, desperate pace. Seconds felt like hours as we scrambled to find anything that might work.

Suddenly Roland jumped up from where he was crouched, searching through a drawer. "What about vitality? That's sort of like healing, right?"

"Give me that," I said, snatching it out of his hand.

The potion called for butterfly wings, dandelion pollen, rock salt, red algae, vinegar, garlic, and pine needles. I nearly threw up in my mouth thinking about drinking the concoction but poor Anne didn't have another option.

I enlisted Roland's help and we went through the cupboards trying to locate the ingredients. Some of them—the ones that dealt with storms, fire, and destruction—were neatly labeled and organized by type. Others, which must have been Mary's, like the dandelion pollen, were haphazardly placed in random locations in no distinguishable order.

"Hey, do you think we could take some of these notes back with us? Like, I'm just saying, an invisibility potion might be useful at home," Roland said as we gathered the supplies.

I had to stop and think about that. Now that I knew what I could do, I could train myself once we were home as long as I had Anne's thorough notes.

"We can't take all of these papers with us," I replied after a moment of careful deliberation.

"Oh, I almost forgot," Roland said, digging around in the pocket of his jeans. "I grabbed your phone while we were in that old guy's house. I didn't think leaving it in the 17th century would be good for anyone. We might go home to spaceships or something."

He held my phone out to me. The decrepit smartphone wasn't good for much, but at least it could take pictures.

"Okay, I'll make the potion. You try to get some photos of what look like the most important notes," I said, turning around to find the last few ingredients.

"And keep in mind, I know pretty much nothing about any of this. So, if it has extra notes written on the side or something, I'll need those too," I continued, realizing that I might be in over my head.

Once I had everything I needed, I tried to follow the instructions. It wasn't like reading a cookbook. The steps didn't seem to be in order. I ground the butterfly wings into dust and mixed them with the other dry ingredients. That part was simple enough. But to combine everything together, Anne's notes called for prayers of thanks to the elements and specific emotions to be felt as each portion was added. I had no clue if it would work or if I was doing it right. I just knew that if I didn't try, not only would I be stuck here for sure, but I might also no longer even exist.

A strange red glow started to emanate from the bottom of the glass goblet as I poured in the last of the vinegar. It crept up the sides slowly, pulsing its way up millimeter by millimeter like a heartbeat.

"I—" I began but stuttered, amazed that I was capable of pulling this off. "I think I've done it."

Roland came over to the wooden table in front of me and gaped at the pulsing fluid.

"Either that or you've created the creepiest and most disgusting cocktail in all of human history," Roland joked as he leaned down to get a better look.

I carefully but hastily carried the concoction back to where Anne lay unconscious in Ezra's lap. He stroked her hair and mumbled so softly to her that I couldn't make out the individual words.

"This might help," I said, holding out the goblet to him.

When he lifted his head to look at me, his eyes were red and brimmed with tears. I had seen that same look in the mirror before. It was the look of someone accepting a loss after they tried so hard to win. My heart went out to this boy. He obviously loved Anne for so much more than her family's charity and kindness.

"Are you sure this will not harm her?" he questioned me; his eyes trained on the pulsing fluid as if it were threatening Anne by just existing.

I knelt down beside him. "I'm not sure of anything, but we can't leave her like this."

"I used to jest with Anne and Mary by saying that Mary was the better sister. Even when we were but babes, Mary was beautiful, happy, carefree. Everything that I sorely lacked." He continued stroking Anne's hair, talking to me but never looking away from her.

"But, Anne… She understood me in ways no one will ever match. She saw my pain, my anger, and instead of weakness, she saw power. Her mother may have provided bread to nourish my body, but Anne nourished my soul."

"Then we have to get her back, Ezra," I said, my voice not much louder than a whisper. I held the cup out to him and he reluctantly took it.

Pressing the rim against her parted lips, he tilted the goblet and the fluid flowed over her lips.

We waited for some sign that it was working, though I wasn't sure what to expect. Would it fill her veins the way reuniting with the amulet had? Would the ground vibrate like it had when she used her magic to disintegrate the door?

But nothing happened. The only sound was the bubbling creek behind us.

My blood ran cold as disappointment washed over me in a wave. Not only because I couldn't harness my magic when it was most important, but because I didn't know how to save her.

Losing her sister and the months of strain had been too much for her young body. Years of living with her counterbalance made her dark magic that much more exhausting to live with now that it was gone.

I sank to the ground. My entire body felt heavy, and I couldn't tell if the wetness on my face was from the lingering sprinkles of rain or tears. Roland came and sat beside me on the damp ground. He took my hand in his, and I didn't have it within me to fight it. I was so tired. Too tired to ignore the part of my heart begging to be comforted. I leaned into him, burying my face in his sweater and let deep gut-wrenching sobs take over me.

He made shushing noises as his hand rubbed circles on my back.

"You did what you could and what no other person could have," he whispered.

Nine

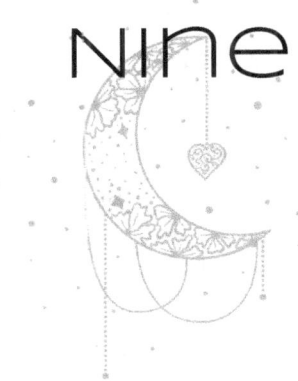

My ears were still pressed between Roland's chest and his bicep, his hold firm and gentle all at the same time when I heard them. Men. Back in the forest, likely a search party. For us? For the dead men from the village? I wasn't sure.

I stood up, wiping my tears away with the sleeve of my leather jacket and walked toward where Anne lay, barely alive, in Ezra's arms. "They are going to pay for this one way or another," I said in a growl.

I reached down and started to lift the amulet over her head. "I'm only borrowing this," I softly whispered in her ear. "You'll have it back before you know it."

The amulet seemed to fight me the entire way. Its tendrils of energy wrapped tight around her waist like a child clinging to its mother and its chain stiffened under my touch. I remembered Anne's words about where its power came from and leaned down to have a stern word with the deceased blessed sisters.

It was a little silly, speaking to a necklace full of my dead ancestors. But once I said, "Please. If I can't save her, at least let me avenge her before I fade away too," the amulet released its hold and came away easily.

I slid it over my own head and its warm power infiltrated my body underneath my skin. The skies darkened above me as my eyes trained on the men breaking through the tree line into the singed meadow. Having lost all track of time, I wasn't sure if it was a storm brewing or twilight setting, but either way, the incoming darkness amplified the energy in my veins.

It was all too much. Too many emotions swirling around in my head. All of my calluses softening and allowing the long-held pain to penetrate. Anne was the only real family I had and now she was gone too. Because of these men. Because of their bigotry.

I felt it all. Every jagged piece of the short stick I had drawn. I was angry, hurt, confused, grieving. The pain in my chest grew and grew until it was hard to breathe. My mind spun and my vision blurred.

My mind kept whispering on its own volition. The darkness was taking hold, its vile poison bubbling up through my consciousness.

They took her away. The only thing you let yourself care about and they ripped her away from you. It isn't fair. What they've done is evil.

Make.

Them.

Pay.

I walked forward, every step a purposeful advancement on the men. I had no plan, but I did have power coursing through my veins. Power like I had never felt before. All consuming, engulfing power. Power that made my skin vibrate and glow a soft purple in the coming darkness.

With every step, my resolve grew stronger and my doubts faded. If the Kane family was to be obliterated from history, then their enemies would be, too.

Kill them all. Right the world's wrongs. They don't deserve mercy they never gave.

If I managed to wipe out all of the witch hunters, then I could save dozens of innocent people. If Anne could hold on long enough, I could wipe out the men in the woods. Then I could go to town and wipe out the judge, the jury, the accusers. Anyone who spread the prejudice and hate that fueled the witch trials.

Nothing but their deaths could quell the fire of rage that roared within me and I felt no guilt because I knew the malice they perpetrated.

You'll feel better once vengeance is served.

The pendant swung toward my back, pulling the chain taut around my neck. My steps faltered. It took all of my strength to move forward. The braided gold dug into my throat, effectively cutting off my airway.

I grabbed at the chain and pulled it back around. "What are you doing? This needs to be done for the good of humanity."

I summoned sparks to my fingertips, readying myself for the battle.

Armor made entirely of dense shadow formed around my body. As I marched, the grass died underneath my feet. The flowers around me started to wilt in my presence.

I was darkness.

I was destruction.

And like the phoenix must be destroyed before it emerges as new, I was going to bring about a better world from the ashes I made of the old.

Now is the time. Unleash your fury upon them so that they will never be able to doubt the powers of darkness.

I raised my hands to the sky, fixed my gaze upon a point in the clouds, and pulled down a swirling twister. With a shove, I sent it barreling in the direction of the men's voices. It quickly tore through the meadow and hit the trees. They cracked as the manifestation of my rage slammed into and through them, clearing its way to the men.

Ezra and Roland's screams for me to stop were barely audible over the roar of the swift-moving wind.

Until they weren't.

The tornado fell apart like butter on a hot knife, clouds melting back up to their original spots in the sky. Still consumed by my anger, I spun on them. Their distraction was the obvious cause of the break in my power.

They stand in the way of your glory, of your peace.

As my body finished its hundred-and-eighty-degree turn, Anne was sitting up, eyes still closed, but with her hand extended toward the woods.

"This isn't the way." Her voice was nothing more than a whisper, but it echoed through my mind like a shout.

The pendant reacted to her voice by pulling me, even harder than before, back toward her. This time I followed it.

The boys looked at me in horror.

I needed them to know I wasn't a monster. "If I can destroy the witch hunters, the trials will stop. Then it will be safe for her here," I pleaded with them to understand.

Roland pointed at my face. "Avery, your eyes!"

"What about my eyes?" I asked. I headed to the creek to see my reflection in its water.

They were solid black. An empty void leading into my mind.

"Why? What?" I sputtered.

Anne roused and stared at me. "You are dangerously close to being consumed by the darkness. You are losing yourself." Her words held no judgment but were filled with concern.

"How do I stop it? Tell me what I need to do." I didn't recognize my own voice as a deep rasp came out instead of my usual timbre.

"I cannot. Each sister must discover her own path to control. Just as every one of us must dive into their darkness alone, so must we surface from it."

"So, do I like think happy thoughts and fly to the second star to the right or something?"

"I've already told you we cannot fly."

Roland laughed and I rolled my eyes. Of course, there was no way she would understand the reference but it summed up the absurdity of how I felt at the moment.

There was a lot of talk about "self-care" and "mental health" in our time. I thought most of it was silly. Bad stuff happens and you keep going. That's how I had survived so far. Taking time to worry about it or pat yourself on the back for getting through it was pointless. There would always be something else that went wrong, something else I had to force myself to survive.

Roland's hand went to my shoulder and he leaned forward to whisper in my ear. "Don't leave me, Avery. Stay with me. Fight it."

And then his arms were wrapped around me, pulling me so close to him that I could feel his pounding heartbeat against my body.

I closed my eyes and fell into his hug, tears threatening to fall from the corners of my eyes as they pressed closed.

My mind told me to fight it.

Told me to push him away.

But I wasn't sure I really wanted to.

I wanted to surrender. To not be strong or hard for a second. I wanted the world to disappear, to let me be a girl falling for a boy. To enjoy the excitement pulsing through me.

But I also knew it wasn't real. Just like the kiss in the cabin, it was only to manipulate my powers. There was no universe in which Roland Bennett, king of Fenway High, would fall for someone like me. This was only an attempt to save his own life, to escape from the hell I put us in.

He pulled back slightly and looked down at me. A grin played at the edges of his mouth.

He was enjoying this a bit too much, the effect he had over me. I still wasn't entirely sure what, if anything, I felt for him. But I couldn't deny the physical response that my body had to his touch.

He turned to Anne and clapped his hands together. "It worked."

Anne looked at me severely. "You cannot always rely on another to center you. You are going to have to learn how to manage your powers on your own."

I threw my hands up in the air in frustration. "I didn't rely on anyone. He did it on his own. I didn't tell him to."

"I understand. But it is easy to be fooled into thinking love will save you. Love is important, yes. But the ability to save yourself is even more important."

I was just happy not to feel the pull of darkness at the back of my mind anymore, to know my thoughts and actions were once again completely my own. There still seemed to be something wrong inside my head though. A strange feeling that something wasn't quite right. A fog settling over all of my thoughts.

The townsmen who ran screaming when the twister appeared showed themselves among the wreckage left behind. Effortlessly, Anne formed a circle of tall flames around them, stopping their advance.

"Why didn't you just do that before?" Roland asked.

"I could not have. Avery made the elixir exceptionally well. I believe I have returned to full strength." She beamed at me with pride, but I was still too shaken to smile back.

"We have to stop them," I said, the anger and determination of moments ago returning.

"No. We don't." She rose from the ground and closed the few feet separating her and the flames surrounding the men. She looked at their shadowed forms through the wall of fire. "There will always be those that are scared of us. If you kill these men, and the men in the village, and every other person who speaks against us, you will only continue a cycle of hate. People will fill the vacancy left in their wake with another form of hate, one that may be even more destructive."

She motioned toward Ezra and began to walk to the cabin. "It's time for Ezra and me to leave. And it's time to send the two of you back home."

She returned from the cabin only moments later, her arms full of colored crystals and jars of various herbs and animal bones. A man screamed from the circle of flames still raging at the corner of the meadow as he tried to escape, nearly burning off one of his legs.

"Oh, hush." Anne flicked her wrist and the flames disappeared, replaced by a funnel of wind. The men tried to escape but were blown around like a shirt in the washing machine. They opened their mouths to scream but any sound was carried away the moment it left their lips. "That's better. Much quieter and not as dreadfully hot."

I stared at her in amazement. I thought that the amount of power I felt pulse through me when I was almost consumed was immense, but that it was only because I let myself take in too much darkness at once.

Anne was now able to lazily and effortlessly throw around her powers like it was nothing, with no obvious strain.

I waved my hands toward the men within the wind funnel. "What even?"

"Your fault was not the amount of emotion; it was your lack of control. The dark is a funny thing. It overtakes your mind and makes you believe that its lies are the truth. This is why you must find a balance. Your sister will help, but you must learn how to tell the difference between using your emotions to amplify your powers and your emotions using you."

She busied herself with arranging the crystals and the other objects in a circle as she spoke. "When you return home, you will find her. Of that, I have no doubt. But you cannot dive headfirst into your powers or else you will lose yourself to them."

I started to walk toward her but she held up one hand to stop me while still looking down at her circle of strange items. "I do not have the time to teach you properly. It will be a hard road for you on your own. But if you walk in the footsteps of your ancestors before you, they will not lead you astray."

"What does that even mean?" I asked. This was not the time for riddles. It appeared that her circle was nearly complete, and the wind funnel she held the men in was starting to thin out.

"You will find out soon enough." She didn't look at me as she rose from the ground and stood in the middle of the circle. "Roland, hold on to her waist."

Roland didn't question her as he slid his warm arms around my middle and held tight. His arms shook slightly, and I didn't know if it was because he was scared of the magic or our closeness.

Dust started to fly up around us as Anne closed her eyes and lifted her hands toward the sky. Clouds formed a thick, dark net in the sky above us. Thunder boomed somewhere in the distance. Anne looked up and her eyes were that same solid black.

"No!" I screamed and tried to break free from Roland's grasp. "She's going to be consumed!"

"Hold her," Anne commanded. Her voice was raspy and cold. It sounded wrong, so unnatural it sent shivers down my spine.

I struggled and twisted and kicked, but nothing would make Roland let go of me. But as I turned to look at him, I saw his eyes too had taken on a dark quality. The sunflowers were now the color of dirt. He didn't say a word. Instead, staring blankly ahead at Anne. It was as if there wasn't a thought in his entire big head.

I held out my hand and a wave of black smoke flew right at Anne's chest. Mere centimeters in front of her, it dissipated instead of knocking her back as I'd intended. Her power was so much stronger than mine. "Ezra, you have to stop her. She's pushing too hard. She's using too much power."

Ezra looked terrified as he cautiously extended one hand over the ring of objects and into the circle. His hand rested gently against Anne's back and her body, which was stiff as a board, visibly relaxed. Her eyes, still dark, showed the tiniest sliver of violet.

"I will be with you always, Avery. Never forget that my love for you is not bound by death nor time."

I wanted to respond but as she finished speaking, one of the men broke free from the weakened wind tunnel and rushed at her.

Anne swiftly glanced in his direction and then right back to me and Roland. She brought her raised hands down to her sides with a swift jerk and a loud roar ripped through the air.

Lightning crashed into me with the force of a semi-truck. I couldn't breathe. I couldn't see. I couldn't feel.

And then I was back in front of her monument outside of the wax museum. As if the past few days had never happened.

Ten

R oland's arms were still around me as I collapsed onto the ground, and I inadvertently pulled him down with me.

"You ok, Avery? Still in one piece?"

He softly turned my head so that I was gazing up at him as he propped himself up on his elbow. The skies had cleared. The shadowy clouds had been replaced with sparkling, clear blue sky.

I took stock of each of my extremities. Nothing felt broken or out of place. At least physically. Mentally was another story.

"I'm fine." I gulped hard to swallow back tears as soon as the words left my mouth. I had been given so many answers about where I came from, who I was, why things happened to me that didn't happen to other people. But they just left more questions. Where was my sister? My parents? How had the Kanes gone from a family of powerful witches to only one lonely girl bouncing from place to place because no one wanted to keep her?

A shout sounded from behind us. "There they are!"

But I didn't look away from Roland. I wasn't ready to deal with anyone else. I wasn't ready to lie or pretend.

"You two stop that this instant." The voice was shouting again, but this time it was directed at me and Roland. I sat up, confused.

The entire sophomore class was now barreling toward us, led by Mrs. Curry.

As she reached us, she leaned down and physically pulled me away from Roland.

"The most disrespectful act I have ever seen. To frolic like this in such a reverent place. I expected more from you, Roland Bennett," she said as she glowered at him.

Giggles floated to my ears from the crowd of students and my pendant warmed against my skin as the embarrassment settled in. I closed my eyes and reveled in its heat as I realized I had it back. It was such a lovely, comforting feeling to have my pendant back. I wrapped my fingers around it, giving it a quick squeeze. Flashes of thunder and lightning filled my mind. I remembered the power coursing through my veins as I pulled a twister straight from the sky.

Make them pay for laughing. Ignite the clouds, crumble the buildings, terrify them so they leave you alone.

The pendant in my hand shook softly and I remembered Anne's words. That was not the way to handle this. The darkness in my mind was loud, but the thoughts weren't my own. If I ignored them, I wouldn't succumb to their power.

I stepped over to where Mrs. Curry had Roland by his shirt collar, lecturing him about respect for the dead and the proper behavior for field trips.

"Mrs. Curry," I said softly. She didn't stop or turn around. She ignored me completely. I cleared my throat and tried again louder, more forcefully. "Excuse me, Mrs. Curry."

This time she wheeled on me. Her rage was suddenly aimed right at me.

"Don't even get me started on you, little miss. You were already on thin ice. No wonder you can never last at a single placement."

Okay, ouch. Did she have to go right for the jugular?

I took a long, slow breath in and forced myself to smile. I wondered briefly if it was within my powers to turn people into toads, or more likely since it was dark magic, wasps; those were definitely evil. Interrupting her, I plead Roland's case.

"Please don't get upset at Roland, Mrs. Curry. I made him come out here with me."

Don't the lies just slide out like silk? Look at how easily deception comes to you. How well it fits you.

The dark pinged at the back of my mind. A pinball threatening to come through as my better-self fought against it. I wanted to use my magic. I wanted to release the dark. But even in attempting to use my own mind instead, the dark was still finding ways to sneak out.

Mrs. Curry shot me a dubious look. The bracelets on her arms rattled against her bony wrists as she led Roland back to the group by the collar.

"Accident or not, your grandmother is going to be so disappointed to find out how you have acted on this trip and the type of people you have started hanging out with."

She left me standing there as if I wasn't even worthy of punishing. I watched as she and Roland melded into the crowd, lost among the masses.

Everything had changed for me, and yet nothing was different. What good was magic when no one sees you, when there was nothing you could do to make your life any better? How was I supposed to hold on to the love that I felt from Anne when there wasn't a soul who cared if I lived or died in the present? Dead ancestors did me no good. I needed real living connections. I needed to know that someone, somewhere, actually gave a crap.

The clear blue sky started pouring rain on top of the entire student body. I knew that I must have subconsciously summoned it. I spread my arms wide and savored its cool bite against my skin. I spun and let it drench every part of me as the drops fell from the sky.

The rest of the class shouted and ran. They hid for cover under nearby awnings or statues and pulled their jackets over their heads. But the rain wasn't heavy or threatening. There was no anger in it. It was sadness. It was longing. It was need.

My mind drifted to Anne's words about finding my sister, about following the footsteps of those that came before me. She was the only one that I knew though, and her story was a dead end. There wasn't even a mention of her inside the museum. At least, not in the part I had been through before my world was turned upside down. Surely, if she was, it would have been with her sister, right? Or maybe, since she wasn't ever hung, there was a separate exhibit for those that were spared.

I needed to get back inside the museum.

I needed to know if she was mentioned.

What happened to her after I left? What happened to Ezra? How could I follow her footsteps if I didn't know where they led? I didn't have much more information about my past than I did before.

ELeven

The rest of my class mulled about in the gift shop, browsing wares depicting ancient Druid symbols and gaudy jewelry. It wasn't difficult to slip by, unnoticed as always.

Inside the exhibit halls, it was dark and quiet. The tour guides must take breaks between groups because there wasn't a soul to be found. The air conditioning turned on overhead and the air whooshed through the halls with an echo. With no one around to see me, I decided this was the perfect time to see if my powers still worked, now that I was back in the present.

I closed my eyes and tried to focus all of my attention on an imaginary point in the center of my chest. I breathed in and out slowly, mindfully, and made a note of each and every feeling in my body. Both the physical and the emotional. The darkness was like a tide coming in as it washed through me. A mental image of black ink staining its way out from the center of my chest until my entire body was little more than shadow came unbidden into my thoughts. I pushed back against it by replacing the image with that of a painter, using his black paint and paintbrush to create a nighttime landscape.

The fury of the darkness settled a bit, centralizing itself into a tingling sensation in my hands. The breeze of the air conditioning played with the tiny hairs on my arms as I moved them this way and that. I reveled in the sensation of becoming one with the air around me and then attempted to mold it to my whim.

A sprinkling of dust on a plaque next to me became my target. If I could manage to clean the dust from the metallic surface, it would prove to me that my powers still worked, without invoking the darkness.

I trained my eyes on the dust, felt the wind leave my body as it flew in the direction of its intended mark. Then, somewhere in the distance, I heard footsteps and laughter.

"I'm telling you, the kid flipped out." I placed the familiar voice as that of our bored tour guide from earlier.

"Geez, Sarah. You would think after working here for so long, you'd learn not to be so superstitious about things," an older male voice replied.

"There's no way she wasn't related though. Those *eyes*." Sarah was clearly more perceptible and interested than I gave her credit for before.

"The Kane sisters are just legends. Ghost stories to keep people coming to the museum." I ducked around the corner and flattened myself against the wall, my back pressing hard against the glass of one of the display cases. I tried to blend into the dim surroundings as much as possible. My only hope was that I could be passed off as a shadow as the tour guides passed.

Before I realized what was happening, I fell backward, landing on my butt at the feet of a terrifying wax judge. His gavel was frozen in mid-swing, no doubt sentencing the scared and wide-eyed wax woman on the floor to certain death. I had somehow ended up inside of the exhibit. Stale air filled my lungs and the lights beat against my skin with an unforgiving harshness. I checked the glass for cracks or openings but found nothing. I managed to phase myself through solid glass without even trying.

"I'm just theorizing here, but what if they were real? We have records of everyone else except them. Maybe that's because they were so powerful, they erased themselves from history."

Now muffled, the voices grew closer. I scrambled across the display's floor and crouched behind the judge's wooden pulpit.

"You're being ridiculous. Don't you think that they would have saved themselves if they were that powerful?"

Saved themselves? As in both of them? The guides seemed to believe that Anne died too. I looked down at my sweaty but tingling fingertips. I was here. I was alive. Which meant that they were wrong. Anne did live, at least long enough to have a child.

Sarah and the other tour guide passed the display I was in without ever looking up. Their backs descended down the hall toward the activity area and their voices floated back to me.

"I mean, what if they didn't die?"

"Isn't it more likely that they never even existed?" the male voice asked, obviously tired of arguing but humoring Sarah.

I needed to hear more, needed to know more. I had to follow them. My options were a small door, camouflaged into the background of the wall behind me, or figuring out how I managed to get myself in here and then try it again.

I knew didn't have time to figure out my powers or how to make them do what I wanted right then so I chose the door.

I turned the knob and carefully cracked it open. I didn't know what lay beyond it, but I knew it wouldn't be somewhere visitors were supposed to be.

The area beyond was just as cold and dark as the exhibit hallway. Large pieces of cloth covered what I could only assume were more wax statues. Brooms, mops, and other cleaning utensils lined the walls. I clumsily made my way through the dimly lit corridor, accidentally kicking over buckets and other objects in my path until I reached a door on the far end of the room.

Echoes of children's laughter and subtle music seeped through the cracks around the door and I silently prayed that no one would see me exit.

The door opened to an area with straw scattered all over the floor. I pressed myself against the wall and slid slowly against the rough surface, the irregular texture scraping my back.

I reached a window with steel bars and chanced a glimpse out of it. Families with kids played with the interactive exhibits, but I saw no museum personnel that might get upset at my trespassing. I searched for an exit. Instead, I only found a door made of iron bars with a chain and padlock keeping it closed.

It suddenly occurred to me that I was stuck inside the mock Salem Witch jail cell. I'd seen it in the brochure. It was just a stage prop really. Meant for the kids to investigate the outside it but not go inside.

This turn of events may have been funny if I had not just escaped an actual jail cell. Now, panic threatened to take hold of me. The darkness pushed against its bounds. It screamed too loud for me to focus on anything else.

Shake the bars loose from their hold. Tear the stones from their foundation. Crumble it. Blow it away. Burn it all to the ground. You could easily be free.

Innocent people would be hurt if I let the darkness take hold and use me for its destruction. I couldn't do it. I could go back into the service hallway and try another exit. But that put me at the risk of being discovered.

I fell into a sitting position, clutching my knees against my chest. Possibilities swarmed in circles inside my head and I tried to pin down the most logical way to get myself out of this situation. If only I knew how I managed to get into that display case to begin with I could do the same now to get out.

I closed my eyes and tried to remember the feeling of hiding in the hallway. If my powers were influenced by my emotions as Anne said, I should be able to recreate them by recreating whatever I'd been feeling.

My biggest goal had been to be unseen, to mesh into the darkness like an ink stain on black paper. I imagined myself as a shadow, nothing more than a cloud in the night sky. My chest began to burn slightly and a tingling sensation washed through my body. I opened my eyes and looked down at my hands, which were now nearly transparent. When I moved my fingers, trails of smoke followed in their path's wake. Tentatively, I stuck my hand through the stone wall of the cell. It passed through easily, like walking through a curtain of water, so I went further, sticking my head out of the wall to see if anyone was around to be freaked out by the shadowy figure emerging from the cell.

My classmates milled about as smaller children ran from one exhibit to the next, all without noticing the translucent girl made of smoke coming out of the walls of the jail cell. As I looked around, Roland's eyes caught mine from his place directly next to Mrs. Curry and my heart skipped a beat. His eyebrows shot up and he started looking around, as if to see if anyone else could see me, but he didn't say a word.

I kept pressing my body through the wall, but now nothing was budging. The wall had solidified around me, or rather I had solidified inside it. With one arm and my head stuck outside the walls of the cell for all the world to see, the other half of my body remained inside.

I looked back up at Roland, now terrified. He saw the pleading in my eyes and scrambled to find a way to get to me without drawing attention to either of us. Sliding in and out between students, smiling, laughing, and generally acting like nothing was wrong, he managed to make his way to me. He put his back to me, facing the crowd in front of us.

"How the hell have you managed this one?" he asked with what sounded like the tiniest bit of annoyance.

"Uh, I fell into one of the exhibits. Apparently, I can turn into a shadow." I struggled against the wall, trying to break myself free.

"Well, you might want to do that again. Quickly." He smiled at some of the other students and pretended to be closely examining the faux brick of the cell.

"I would love to," I growled back.

"Then what is the issue? Just do it like you did it before."

Once again, I tried to pull on my memories of hiding in the hallway, of turning myself into a spot of blackness. But there was no pain in my chest, no tingle in my finger, and definitely no wispy smoke body.

"It's not working like it did before. All I had to do was think about not wanting to be seen and it worked. Now when I try, nothing." I waved my arms in frustration, but only the one stuck inside the cell moved.

"Do you think it might be because you want to be seen?" He chanced a glance in my direction.

"That's ridiculous. The last thing I want to do is explain to Mrs. Curry how the hell I got myself stuck inside the wall."

"Never mind," he said as he shook his head.

The moment I saw Roland was the moment I solidified. *Were the two related? Did I truly want Roland to see me so badly that it canceled out my magic?*

"I'm here, Avery. I'm not going anywhere. No matter how weird things get. So just get your funky monkey butt out of that wall before we get in trouble."

I laughed him off, but his words hit deep. There was no one in my life that was willing to put up with how weird things could get around me. No one who was willing to stay.

The boy lies. He will leave. They all leave.

Deep down I knew they were just words Roland said to make himself feel better, to get out of this dilemma, to get *me* out of this dilemma. But I wanted to believe him so badly that I nearly let myself think that he would stay. That he really didn't mind my strangeness.

I summoned my need for invisibility one more time. Roland's body stiffened as his hand fell slightly once my cheek was no longer solid. Before I could solidify again, I yanked my entire body out of the wall. My sneakers caught and I had to tug hard to pull them free.

I landed on my hands and knees at Roland's feet and quickly stood up.

"One of these days I'm going to be able to do that without bruising something," I quipped as I dusted off my black jeans.

"One of these days we're actually going to get to shower," Roland replied, sniffing at his shoulder for emphasis. "How long has it been?"

I pulled my fingers through my hair that was now soaked in grease and dirt from the 17th century. "Not nearly as long as it feels."

The smirk he gave me in return made my knees sway a bit underneath me and I had to put my hand on his elbow to balance myself.

"You need to get some rest," he said as he pulled me forward. "And food. When's the last time you ate?"

"Ezra brought bread to the cell the first day I was there." Saying his name out loud felt strange, this orphan boy from the sixteen hundreds. What became of him? Did he escape his unfortunate circumstances? Did he follow Anne wherever she was escaping to?

Roland led me to a bench against the wall and sat me down. He slung his backpack around to the front of his hips and started to unzip it.

"How did that thing manage to survive?" With all we had been through, that stupid canvas bag looked like it was in better shape than we were.

"No idea. But the plus side is we still have snacks." He pulled a stick of jerky out of one of the pockets and held it out to me.

"Do you always keep a never-ending supply of jerky in your backpack? It's a wonder all the dogs in town don't follow you around constantly." I took the jerky and started to slowly peel away the plastic wrapping.

Roland focused hard on removing the wrapping of his own. "My grandmother puts it in here for field trips."

I imagined a chubby old lady with white hair carefully packing food and water in her grandson's backpack so that he wouldn't go hungry on his outing. It must feel wonderful to have someone who was willing to go out of their way for you like that. Someone who thought of you and your well-being.

"Curry mentioned your grandmother earlier. Does she know her or something?" I had spent five days a week around this boy but still knew so little about him outside of the classroom.

"I mean, they aren't friends or anything." He stood up from his perch in front of me and looked away from me as he took a bite of jerky.

"Okay?" That wasn't an answer. He looked down at me, something in his gaze telling me the situation was complicated. He sat down next to me and leaned back against the wall.

"My granddad died last year. It's just me and Gran now. There wasn't enough money for school supplies so Curry covered them. Now she holds it over my head any time I even think about stepping out of line."

I knew better than to ask where his parents were. The first rule of foster kids, if they don't talk about their parents, is don't ask about them. It was never anything those kids would want to rehash during small talk.

"Your gran sounds amazing," I said, placing my hand on his knee for comfort.

He looked down at it thoughtfully. "She tries" was his only response before Mrs. Curry walked by and squinted at me. I carefully removed my hand from Roland's knee and placed it on my own.

"I think there's information here about Anne," I whispered to Roland once a crowd of students walked by and Curry got distracted by some kid who accidentally knocked over podium holding an old book.

"Yeah, I saw it when I walked into the activity center. How did you miss it?"

"I didn't exactly enter through the front door."

Roland rested his head against the wall, his eyes closed. The poor kid needed some sleep, but after all that happened, I needed answers.

TweLve

A painting hung on the wall at the entrance to the activity center. Two silhouettes, one in shades of white, the other in shades of black. Below them, a gold engraved plaque read:

The Mysterious Kane Sisters

According to legend, the Kane sisters, Mary and Anne, lived with their mother several miles outside of Salem Village, but the exact location is unknown.

Mary Kane was the supposed first victim of the Salem Witch Trials. Reports of seeing her grow flowers instantly set the town into the frenzy that cost twenty people their lives.

Anne Kane, who was apprehended at the same time, somehow escaped the Trials.

For the thrill-seekers among us, it is said that when both the sun and moon are in the sky, you can follow their footsteps to the top of Gallows Hill and hear Anne cry for her sister. But BE WARNED: if you stay too long, she will mistake you for her sister's hangman and freeze your bones where you stand.

"Follow the footsteps of those that came before."

Those were the exact words that Anne said to me just before she sent me back. This had to be what she meant. It felt like a clue.

Too easy. Nothing in your life comes this easily. Don't believe it.

I ran back to Roland, still half asleep on the bench. "How do I get to Gallows Hill?" I was out of breath and a little manic.

He sat up, blinking the sleepy haze from his eyes.

"Avery, that's all the way across town."

"Anne left me clues there." The sentence jumbled into one long word.

"I read the plaque too. But the sun and the moon both have to be in the sky, and we have no way to get there."

"There has to be a way." I sounded like a petulant child. I *was* a petulant child. I needed to know more, and I wasn't going to wait.

"Unless you can fly—"

I glared at him and he stopped speaking. He knew that was a touchy subject. If I was going to have powers, I wanted to be able to fly. Like Sabrina, or even those witches from Hocus Pocus who flew on mops and vacuums.

"Look, let's just survive the rest of this field trip, go home and take a shower and sleep in a warm, nice twenty-first century bed, and then we can go explore Gallows Hill later."

The bed thing did sound nice. My bones still ached from the hard surface of the jail cell floor, not to mention all the tumbles I had endured in the past seventy-two hours. Was it seventy-two hours? Did it still count if you arrived back at the same moment when you left?

"How are we going to get back here? It's nearly an hour drive." No matter how good my bed and a shower sounded, my need for answers was greater.

"There are buses. Taxis. Ubers."

I knew he was right, but I was impatient. It was my turn to sit down on the bench dejectedly.

"How long do we have before we go home?" I asked, my tone deadpan.

"It doesn't seem like we were gone more than about thirty minutes."

"So, in theory, we still have a couple of hours before the buses leave, right?"

"Avery."

"Just hear me out." I was begging. I knew I was begging. But I didn't care. "If we wait until lunchtime when everyone scatters, we could order an Uber, go to Gallows Hill, and get back here before they even notice we're gone."

Roland finally sat up straight, pulled his hoodie back from his head, and looked me in the eyes. "Curry would notice. And even if we could — even if we didn't get caught and suspended or worse, the moon and sun won't be in the sky at the same time."

"Maybe I could fix that." I smiled and wiggled my shoulders.

Roland looked at me like I knew better. "With your lack of control over your powers, we'd be safer if we waited until sunset."

I playfully slapped at his arm. "Hey, it isn't easy harnessing literal darkness and channeling it into controlled chaos. You should try it sometime and see how well you can handle it."

"Oh, wow, can you hear yourself? This morning I would have petitioned to put you in some sort of asylum for talking like that. Give it a day for everything to settle in at least, Avery."

Mrs. Curry walked by, sending more daggers in my direction. I thought about returning the glare, but I was scared mine would form into actual daggers.

"We are leaving now. If you two can behave long enough to join the group and make your way to the Witch Village, it would be appreciated."

Roland and I looked at each other, our shared secret creating a bond I could no longer deny.

"Let's do this, I guess," Roland said, standing up and taking my hand.

He held it through the rest of the field trip. I told myself it was to make sure I didn't try to run away to Proctor's Ridge, not because he wanted to, but every now and again his stolen glances and sideways smiles sent my heart and my head into overdrive. He really was beautiful. I was starting to see why everyone at school loved him. I could easily see myself doing the same if he kept looking at me like that.

But he wouldn't. No one ever did. I knew better than to let myself fall into a false sense of security with him. Things in my life were even crazier than usual right now. I needed to get that under control. I needed to find my sister. I needed to know what happened to Anne after we left. But I wanted to think about him instead. I wanted to look at him, to touch him. He was a danger to my plans. He was poison to my emotions and I couldn't afford to have them go haywire when they were already threatening to take over.

That night when Lynne picked me up, her minivan already loaded with the other two temporary children, I didn't say a word.

Not that I had much chance. Olivia was already deep into the retelling of her day from beginning to end, not leaving out a single detail.

No one noticed I didn't speak.

No one cared.

I told myself it was better that way. Once I found my sister, I wouldn't have to bother them for attention anymore. Not that I asked for much.

I was a liability.

Unstable.

More so now than ever before. I let myself blend into the background through dinner and their nightly bedtime routine.

They wouldn't even notice if you had stayed in the past. Being here only makes things more difficult for them. You're just another mouth to feed.

There were only two bedrooms in the small, worn-down townhome. Lynne slept in one while a set of bunk beds and one toddler bed were crammed into the other. But Olivia hardly ever slept on the smaller bed. Every night after Lynne put her to sleep, she would get up and drowsily find her way to the foot of Lynne's bed.

My bottom bunk wasn't much more comfortable than the cell floor, but I was happy to see it at the end of the day. I laid there in the dark, staring at the bunk above mine where Alison snored, as I transferred sparks from one finger to the next. The door cracked open slightly and my foster mom stuck her head in.

"You okay, Avery?" she asked in a sugary sweet tone. "You haven't spoken much since we picked you up."

I hid my hands underneath my covers as if she could see the magic lingering on them. Her dark skin shimmered in the moonlight from the window like black silk and micro braids framed her bony face. She looked worn, like life had given her one too many hurdles to jump.

"I'm fine. Just tired."

She sat down on the edge of the bed and studied me with a look I knew all too well. She was kind, but she was just another foster mom. All good things came to an end. And this was a fitting end for my time here. It had been a good run. I couldn't be upset that it was over. Lynne had already given me more than any other adult in my life ever did.

"It's time for me to go. Isn't it?" I asked after a couple of moments of silence.

My words seemed to age her, and I knew what the answer would be before she spoke.

"Avery," she started, her voice low and sorrowful.

"No, it's fine. I understand how these things go." My own voice was tight and clipped, trying to hold back tears.

"Avery, stop. I didn't come to tell you that you have to leave."

The shock must have been evident on my face because her expression brightened a bit.

"You have a home here. For as long as you want it."

She is spoon feeding you lies. You will never have a home.

I blinked rapidly, trying to clear the darkness from my eyes and hopefully my mind.

She reached forward as if she was going to touch my cheek. The gesture made me ache for the same kindness and affection Anne had shown me in the cell, but when she was less than an inch away, she pulled her hand back and awkwardly folded it in her lap.

You disgust her so much that she cannot even touch you.

"I know that it hasn't been easy for you, Avery. But I want to change that. You're a good kid, and smart. I want you to feel like you belong here. You should know you can talk to me about anything. I'm always here for you."

Why did people keep saying that? First Roland and now her. I knew better. Everyone who said it before ended up leaving. The saying didn't hold much ground for me and, as far as placations went, it was pretty unimaginative. I could see her child psychology degree earning its worth behind her eyes. I wasn't a puzzle to be pieced together or to study under a microscope. The whole interaction made me want to squirm, but I forced a smile.

"Thanks."

She got up and walked to the door, turning around to lock at me as she shut it behind her. I kept the plasticine smile in place until the door was fully closed and then rolled my eyes and went back to playing with my sparks.

I slept hard. Too hard. By the time I woke up, the sun was blazing through my window and the clock on Alison's dresser told me it was nearly afternoon.

I groggily walked down to the kitchen to ask why no one woke me up. The darkness told me it was because they didn't care if I died in my sleep, but I wanted to prove it wrong. The house was eerily absent of the sounds of screaming children that usually occupied it as I poured cereal into a bowl and sat down at the kitchen table across from Lynne, who was dutifully clipping coupons.

"Where's everybody else?" I asked as I shoveled the puffed corn pieces into my mouth.

"Olivia and Ali went to the park."

"Why didn't you wake me up?"

"You seemed like you needed the rest after yesterday."

I tilted my head slightly, my eyes shifting to the side while I tried to figure out why she was acting so strange.

"You know, the only thing I ever wanted was to be a mom."

Now I was seriously out of my depth. Warm, fuzzy conversations were not my strong suit. I could talk music or science all she wanted, but this was weird. Lynne didn't ever talk about herself or her past. I didn't need to know more about her than I already did. Lynne took in damaged kids and fed them and I was a damaged kid that needed feeding. It was a good deal. At least for as long as I could keep it.

"We got married right out of college and I thought we would start a family immediately. But fate had other plans. We tried for years. We were getting ready to start infertility treatments when he was in his car accident."

I visibly winced but didn't say a word and let her continue because, clearly, she needed to tell this story to someone.

"He was in a coma for three months before he passed. At first, his family was very supportive. They called and checked on me. They would send food or gifts. Eventually, I guess it got too much for them to be around someone that was constantly so depressed. The rest of my friends followed suit and gave up on me shortly after."

My cereal bowl was empty, but I didn't get up to refill it. She looked so vulnerable, so delicate, that I was scared any movement might break her.

"I can't blame them. Everything was so dark in those days. I lost the only things I ever wanted for myself, the love of my life and a chance at a family. I walked around for years in a gray haze, unable to truly connect with anyone on a real level."

I knew that feeling. Now we were talking my language. I knew depression and sadness well, but I didn't have any advice to make it better or deal with it if that was what she was looking for.

Sob story, the darkness snarked in the back of my mind. *She doesn't want to feel guilty when she tells you that she is returning you. This is all for her own sick gratification.*

"Somehow, I managed to keep my job, which was probably a failure on my boss' end." She laughed but it sounded hollow. "Kids would come in day after day and their problems were so much worse than mine."

I shifted uncomfortably, unsure how to respond.

"I know, I know. Pain is relative. And that's true, but some of these kids were facing problems I couldn't wrap my brain around even as an adult. But they kept going. You guys are resilient little things, ya know."

She stopped clipping her coupons and looked up at me with twinkling eyes. My own eyes shifted to my empty bowl, unable to fully meet her gaze. I wasn't resilient. I was broken. She was wrong.

"My practice was tasked with evaluating foster kids as they came through the system." She kept her eyes down this time but put the scissors on the table. "Kids like you who have been bounced around for years. And the only thing I ever found wrong was that they needed someone who saw how amazing they were and wouldn't give up on them. That's when I decided that I had too much love to give, and they had too great a need for love, for me to keep it from them. That's why I do this." She waved her hand around the room, indicating the messy kitchen and the kids' art all over the walls. "You guys saved me."

"Saved" did not seem to be the right word. She still didn't have what she wanted. She was single with three foster kids, a minivan that was on its last leg, and a townhouse that was falling apart. Not exactly the American dream.

The doorbell rang and we both jumped and looked at each other, confused. Lynne went into the living room to open the door and I took the chance to refill my bowl.

"Avery, darling, were you expecting someone?" Lynne asked as she walked back into the room. Roland peeked his head out from behind her and I nearly spit out my mouthful of cereal.

I looked down at my black tank top and boxer shorts and wished I had thrown on some jeans, at least, before I came down for breakfast.

"I thought I would surprise her." Roland turned the charm up to one hundred as he beamed at Lynne. "Avery mentioned wanting to join our study group yesterday and I thought I would see if she wanted to go with me. We're going discuss the witch trials in further detail today."

Oh, he was so good at lies.

Lynne smiled sweetly and gave me a knowing look. "Promise to have her back before bedtime?" she asked him, all but giving me permission.

THIrTeen

An old blue Buick Park Avenue sat running in my driveway. The noises coming from its engine sounded like it had barely made it here in one piece.

"I thought we were going to Uber," I said as I opened the passenger door and got in.

"Nan's having one of her bad days. She won't even notice the car's missing."

One of her bad days? The way Roland avoided eye contact told me he didn't want to talk about it, so I didn't ask.

He doesn't want to tell you because he knows you will eventually use it against him. You know how and where to hit people the hardest.

"I couldn't sleep last night after we got back. Which made absolutely no sense because I was exhausted. But something about the legend was bothering me," he said as he pulled out his phone and tapped at it.

"Here." He shoved the phone toward me and I took it. On it, an article from the Salem News showed an old man in front of some trees. "The top of Gallows Hill is called Proctor's Ledge. In 2016, a study found that it is the exact site of the executions, not the memorial like many previously thought."

"Okay… I'm guessing there is more to it than that."

"Legend says that you have to follow her footsteps. Back in the day, you couldn't exactly take a car up there. And if we want to do this exactly like the legend says we're going to have to do some walking."

Thank goodness I could only find my boots in my hurry to get dressed and get out the door.

"Walking or hiking?" My muscles were still tired from the previous day, even after sleeping half the day away.

"Walking. It's been hundreds of years. The town has grown up around the historical markers. For instance, the original memorial site for Proctor's Ridge is pretty much in the back parking lot of a Walgreens."

I raised one eyebrow. "Seriously? They put a drug store on the site where all of those people died?"

"In their defense, it wasn't known that they were hung at Proctor's Ridge until recently. Now it's in the middle of a neighborhood. Can you imagine the ghost stories those people could tell?"

"So how do we follow her footsteps? Where do we start?"

He reached over and slid the picture of the old man to the left. A sketch of a hillside took its place.

"That's what we're looking for, only three hundred some odd years later." He slid the picture again to now show a topographical map detailing where old roads once existed. "That's our key to finding it. We will follow the path from the old jail site to the ridge."

"So, it's like a treasure hunt, only instead of finding gold, we might find a ghost that wants to freeze our bones. Sounds fun," I quipped. Roland shook his head subtly and pulled the car out of the driveway.

The drive to Salem was peaceful as I sorted through the rest of the research on his phone. The boy must have stayed up all night making sure we were on the right track. There was a Google Doc full of research notes, a map of current day Salem, and multiple maps of old Salem Village. I stole glances at him from time to time when I knew he wouldn't catch me. I couldn't figure out why he was helping me. The darkness tried to tell me it was to laugh when this all exploded in my face, but I hoped it was more than that.

A cop pulled out behind us on the interstate and Roland drew his shoulders back to sit straight as a board.

"What's wrong?"

"Nothing." His hands gripped the steering wheel so tightly his knuckles were turning white.

"You don't have a license, do you?"

"Not technically. I don't turn sixteen until next month," he mumbled.

"Roland Bennett, you rebel." I smiled at him proudly.

"You're gonna be hell for my criminal record, Avery Smith." And there was that smile that made me weak again and, in its wake, the darkness tried to pull me back under. It always seemed to get worse after I allowed myself to be happy for a few moments. As if it couldn't stand the threat of other, positive emotions taking over and giving me peace.

Hear that? You're bad for him. He already knows it. You destroy everything you touch. He won't be the exception. If you really like him, let him go.

The cop went around us. Roland relaxed back into the seat, and I decided to close my eyes and fall asleep. I couldn't handle the darkness right now. I didn't want to be me for a while. And until someone figured out how to turn off the brain without turning off the body, the closest I could come to that was sleep.

I jerked awake as a stranger's tinny voice broke the silence. "Welcome to Burger King. How can I serve you?"

I looked over at Roland and cleared the sleep from my eyes.

"Really?" I mouthed.

"One moment," he said into the speaker. "What? We need food for the trip. Might as well get some nuggs."

"Nuggs?"

"Nuggs."

He ordered a ridiculous amount of chicken nuggets, fries, and two huge drinks and pulled into a parking spot once he had his food.

"Okay," he said with a mouth full of processed chicken. "We know that the jail used to sit on what is now St. Peter Street." He pointed at a star on the map of current day Salem. "We can park there and walk up this street." He moved his finger to a long, highlighted road called Bridge Street. "Take a left on Boston Street and then we should see the Walgreens."

I looked out the window to the heavy amount of traffic buzzing past as I munched on a fry. "How far up the street are we talking?"

"Relax, it's only about a twenty-minute walk."

"I think that's going to be easier said than done."

He smiled behind his eighth chicken nugget and pulled back out on the road.

I stared at him for a beat too long, trying to put the pieces together before I got up the courage to just ask him what was on my mind.

"Why are you helping me?"

He snuck a glance at me before looking back at the road and grinning. "Morbid curiosity maybe."

Sighing, I put my head into my hands.

"Okay, fine. You honestly want to know?"

I sat back up to look at him. "Would I have asked if I didn't?"

His smile widened. "You shouldn't have to do this alone."

I turned away from him and stared at the shopping mall we were passing. "I'm fine alone. I don't need you to protect me."

He laughed. "As if I could. You're the main character. I'm here for comic relief."

Maybe I could live with that. Maybe that could be okay.

You'll eat him alive.

He steered the car into the shopping mall's parking garage and found a spot.

Before we got out, I turned to him, hoping to level with him one last time before he bound his fate to mine any more than he already had.

"You act like you haven't heard the rumors, the whispers, the taunts. You act like you have no idea what you're getting into. I'm dangerous to be around, Roland. You've seen it yourself."

His smile didn't falter as he put his hand on top of mine where it rested between us. "You aren't your reputation and you aren't your magic. You're Avery. You're weird, and unique, and wicked smart."

I lowered my head and closed my eyes.

Lies.

"Don't let me break you."

He took his hand from on top of mine and lifted my chin with a single finger. "As long as you don't break yourself."

With the silent agreement between us, we headed down Saint Peter Street on foot. Next to a set of luxury apartments, Roland jerked to a halt and stared at the building.

"Hard to recognize it now," he said.

"What?" I looked around to see what he could possibly be talking about.

"That is, or was, the jail. Where I thought you were going to die."

I resumed walking. We couldn't let my past brush with death distract us from our goal. Roland didn't follow. He just continued to stand there, staring at the building as if it were a dinosaur in the middle of the city. If I wasn't mistaken, there were little bits of moisture accumulating under his non-blinking eyes.

"We can't focus on that. We have to keep going." I grabbed his arm and started to pull him down the street.

"Avery, just take half a second and look around. Don't you feel the weight of it all?"

I didn't want to fight with him, but we needed to keep moving before we ran out of time. "There is no weight to feel. Now it's just like every other street in every other town."

"But it isn't. You saw it first-hand. What it was. What happened here. How can you just walk past this stuff after that?"

"Ignorance make life easier, Roland. Without it, I would have died a long time ago. Evil doesn't surprise me anymore. Kindness does. So, you'll excuse me if the people of Salem Village lived up to my expectations." He drove me insane. I wasn't going to lay out my pitiful life story for him, but I had every reason not to be shocked that those men who imprisoned me thought those that were different or strange should be punished. "That it does surprise you tells me everything I need to know about how easy your life has been, just because you're cute and smart."

That got his attention. His eyes widened and he fixed his eyes on me, finally.

"You think I'm cute?"

I let out a disgusted sigh. "Don't let it go to your head. I also think you're the most irritating boy on the planet."

"But, like, adorably irritating, right?" He started walking toward me and I moved back a couple of steps. It occurred to me that if I kept goading him, I might be able to get him moving again without having to drag him down the sidewalk.

"More like painfully irritating." Another two steps backward.

He followed. "You didn't seem to mind too much on the field trip."

"Yeah, well, exhaustion can make people do strange things." Two more steps and half of a third before my heel caught on a crack in the sidewalk. My leg buckled beneath me and I started to tumble backward. Roland threw his arm around me just in time to catch me from falling on my back in the middle of the traffic-riddled street. He pulled me up to face him.

"Too busy trying to keep me moving to even look where you're going. I think you've had enough close encounters with death this week," he said, tucking a lock of hair that was dangling in front of my face behind my ear.

I pulled away from him and shook the lock of hair loose. "I was fine. I would have caught myself." I stomped away from him to the crosswalk. "We need to go. We're losing time."

He motioned to the cars in front of me and the DO NOT WALK symbol on the sign across from us. "Well, maybe this time you should wait until you aren't going to get run over?"

I squinted at him, and my teeth ground together. He put his hands up in surrender and backed away.

"Mood swings much," he mumbled under his breath. I pretended not to hear him and started walking across the street as the light changed.

Roland walked a couple of steps behind me the rest of the way up Bridge Street. The sidewalks started deteriorating and the huge cement buildings gave way to rundown shops and old abandoned factories. Eventually, the sidewalk narrowed so much that I was scared we would be hit by a car's side mirror as we walked.

"Roland, quit moping and get up here. Now it's you that's trying to get hit by a car." I called out behind me.

He shuffled quickly to close the few feet between us.

"You summoned, my lady," he said with a ridiculous bow.

Just then an SUV nearly clipped another car and came careening toward the place Roland was just standing. Brakes squealed and the smell of burnt rubber filled my nose. A sharp pain in my chest sent me to my knees at Roland's feet as metal groaned and crunched against the concrete embankment and glass sprayed around us in a crystalline explosion.

I couldn't breathe. I couldn't move. The pain was searing, radiating from my chest through my veins and over my entire body. My life flashed before my eyes, just like people in movies said it would. But there was something else too. Something that was even more of a gut punch than the countless slamming doors and crippling loneliness of my childhood.

The future I let myself hope for since meeting Anne was in between the flashes. If I was being completely honest with myself, I'd let myself hope for it since getting forced into that stupid science experiment with Roland. The pain and grief of a life I'd never get to live if I died on this sidewalk pulsed through me. A life where people waited up for me, where people texted to make sure I was okay, where people told me I was unique. A future where people loved me.

I weakly lifted my hand to my chest and then pulled it away, expecting to find it blood-soaked. But there was nothing. Heavy drops of water fell to the pavement below me and I was surprised to find they were my own tears.

The ringing in my ears started to subside and then Roland was screaming and pulling at my arms. "Avery, get up!"

I looked up at him to find we were encircled in a violet sphere, coming from my amulet.

"We've gotta get out of here before people start asking questions," he said as he threw one of my arms around his shoulders and started to lead me away.

I didn't speak but turned just enough to look back at the wreckage. A spray of metal and glass formed a perfect circle in the place where we had stood and the rear corner of the SUV was collapsed in, as if it had been hit with a wrecking ball.

The owner of the SUV opened the door and started pointing in our direction so I pulled Roland to the other side of a fence and started running.

"My chest hurts," I said as soon as we were far enough away from the accident and I was sure no one was after us. "It's never hurt like that before. I could have sworn I was impaled by something."

"I don't think you've ever tried anything that big before. I mean, you made a shield around us. That couldn't have been easy."

The Walgreens came into view as we spoke but we didn't slow down. "I didn't even try though. It wasn't me who made it."

He looked over at me as if that was the craziest thing I'd ever said, when I knew for a fact, it was not even in the top ten after the week we'd had. "Then who was it?"

"I think it was *them*. Anne and whoever else is in here." I motioned at the amulet laying on my chest.

Roland and I rounded the corner to the back parking lot, and he stopped. He looked between my face and the amulet, but whatever he was thinking about my theory, he didn't say it out loud. "It should be right on the other side of this house behind us."

"I don't know, Roland. This doesn't feel right. Shouldn't the crystal light up or something?" I tapped at it with my index finger as if it was a broken watch.

"How do we know it has anything to do with the amulet? We don't know what we'll find. We've already come all this way."

I started walking again, but slowly, scared that this entire trip would be for nothing. Worried that my only lead to Anne would be an urban legend meant to scare children. Worried that my only hope of feeling whole would be washed away without fanfare. Just another broken dream drifting away on the breeze.

Fourteen

W e passed the single house between the drug store and a small semi-circular concrete area with a seedling tree in front. As we approached, it didn't take long to see the names on the wall were already fading, even though Roland told me this monument was fairly new. I took each step deliberately, waiting for something to happen, but nothing did.

"This doesn't seem right. Why would they pick this place to execute them? The hillside isn't even that steep," I said, double checking Roland's map.

"It wasn't about steepness. No one wants dead bodies cluttering up their town. So, they went just outside the town line to hang them. That river we walked by? It was the town line. They crossed it and then found the first place a cart could reach with a ledge."

I shuddered, thinking of the innocent people that were transported to meet their demise. I read the names of each victim out loud, giving remembrance to each one in the best way I could.

"Higher." I couldn't tell if Roland talking to me or if it someone else close by.

"Did you say something?" I turned and asked him.

He looked confused. "Uh, no. I haven't said a word."

"Higher," the whisper came again.

"See. There. Just now. Someone said higher."

He looked around, walked the length of the half circle wall that made up the concrete and stone monument, and came back to me.

"It's just us here," he said with concern.

I was already halfway up the stones before I turned back to him. "I'm climbing the ridge." I pulled myself up onto the green grass at the top of the four-foot wall.

He motioned to a metal sign posted near the base of the wall. "Avery, it specifically says not to climb the ridge."

I lifted one shoulder in a shrug as I straightened back up. "I've never been great at following instructions."

Roland sighed before scaling the wall and starting up the embankment with me. We climbed through the sparse clusters of trees and boulders until a black chain link fence stopped us from going into someone's backyard.

I looked down at my amulet. Still nothing.

"Patience," the whisper said again.

"Ugh, please tell me you're hearing it now. I really don't want to be going crazy."

"That ship has already sailed," Roland said with a smirk and a wink.

I responded again with squinting and gritting my teeth. I was going to make him pay my dental bills if he kept this up.

"Regardless, what is the mystery voice in your head telling you?" he asked.

"Patience."

"See, it likes me. It wants you to quit giving me such a hard time." He shimmied his shoulders.

"I hardly think that's the case. Lest you forget, you were not exactly Anne's favorite," I said with a smile, remembering how she nearly bit his head off when he interrupted my storm making.

"She would have grown to love me. I know it. Look." He pointed at the sky. It was growing darker, the sun lowering itself into an array of colors in the west and night falling on the east. Though you couldn't see the celestial body over the roofs of the nearby houses and the scattered trees, the effects it painted in the sky were unmistakable.

"If something is going to happen, now would be the time," I called out to the disembodied voice.

Nothing.

Roland's eyes softened as he took my hand. "It's gonna be okay. Maybe this wasn't what you were looking for, but we will find your sister somehow."

I pulled my hand back out of his. "How, Mr. Optimism? Do you have any ideas on where to find her? Because this was it. This was the only clue I had."

He tried to put his arm around my shoulder but I ducked out of it, skirting around him and nearly running into a nearby tree. I put my back to it and slid down, my hands cupping my head.

You'll never find her. You are destined to walk alone. It's better for her that way. At least you won't be able to drag her down with you.

A pull at my neck made me jerk my head away from my hands. The amulet was glowing again.

"Higher."

"Thank goodness," Roland said with a sigh of relief as he stared at the violet glow. "You were going to be miserable to deal with on the car ride back if this didn't work."

The amulet pulled forward on its chain and I took it from around my neck to loop it around my hand.

"Shut up and just follow the darn thing," I said as I started walking in the direction it was guiding me.

Another concrete path led us higher and higher up the hill and away from the monument.

"Higher."

"I'm going!" I yelled back but Roland looked at me with raised eyebrows.

"The voice again?"

I just hung my head and let out a breath. The hill was killing me. It was so steep, and my muscles burned with every step, but the amulet kept pulling and I kept walking until we were in the parking lot of a huge, brick, multi-level building.

"Higher," the whisper said.

I stared at the outside walls, peppered with windows. "Seriously? How am I supposed to get up there?"

"Seems like we're breaking onto a roof now. Is that correct? I am only getting one side of this conversation, after all," Roland said.

"You aren't missing much. It isn't that talkative. Higher seems to be the word of the day." The strange was becoming commonplace and I was slowly losing all sense of how utterly insane this all was.

Getting into the building was easy enough. We just had to wait until someone came out and then go in before the door closed. Thank the crystal there was no doorman.

Finding roof access was harder. We pressed the elevator button for the top floor, but it opened to another floor with a long hallway full of similar looking doors. There was no obvious door that led to a staircase for the roof. Another dead end.

"There's got to be some way to get up there," I said as we walked through the hall one more time, checking each door as we went.

"Probably some sort of service elevator that we haven't found."

"Unhelpful."

"Can you like—" he wiggled his fingers at my necklace "—magic it?"

"Still not helpful," I replied. What good was my magic in a scenario like this? I could harness darkness and destruction. But I needed to be able to climb onto a roof. Those were two really different things. And after the pain in my chest from the shield, I was more than content with sticking to weak, little sparks from now on.

"Seriously though, you can phase through walls, Avery. Quit acting like you don't realize how powerful you are."

I spun to face him, balling my hands into fists. "Roland, do you not realize what using my magic does to me? It hurts.

And not just that, I have to worry about being consumed. Is that what you want?"

You know it is.

His expression shifted quickly from shock to concern. "I didn't think about that. I'm… I'm really sorry."

I shook my head and tried to clear out the darkness screaming inside it.

"No, you're right," I said after a moment. "There's got to be something I can do."

I pressed my ear against one of the doors and listened for signs of life inside. Not hearing any, I pulled on my magic tentatively, dipping my toe into the blackness without jumping in head first. My hand started to fade, and the shadow crept up my forearm. The pull of darkness resounded in my head like the crack of a whip, and I steeled myself against its onslaught of intrusive thoughts.

Before I could question myself, I stuck my hand through the door and turned the lock on the inside. Opening the door slowly, I walked in as stealthily as I could.

It was very obviously the home of a young bachelor. Video game controllers and pizza boxes littered the floor and a layer of dust coated everything in sight. It smelled slightly earthy, and not in a good way. Fortunately, the condo lacked any signs of life and I went straight for the window at the back of the living room.

"Crap, no fire escape," I said as I pulled up the blinds.

Roland laughed. "I could have told you that. Did you not look at the building on the way in?"

"I'm going to have to climb," I said, opening the window.

"You're going to what? Oh, hell no. Have you lost it?" Roland jumped between me and the window, blocking my path.

"I've got to get up there." I tried to maneuver around him but he was bigger than me and he moved faster.

"You'll kill yourself." He grabbed my shoulders and forced me to look at him.

"I'll die knowing I tried then."

"Avery," he begged.

"I can do this. Don't ask me how, but I know I can." It wasn't entirely the truth. I was terrified. I absolutely doubted that I could do it. The height alone made my legs feel like wet spaghetti noodles. I couldn't even walk backward on a sidewalk without tumbling into oncoming traffic. How did I think I could possibly scale a building? But my need for answers was greater than my fear of heights. We came so far. I wasn't stopping now, even if it did kill me.

What would it matter? Who would care? Dying would be a release.

"There's got to be another way," Roland pleaded. "Don't do this. We'll find another way. Some other clue to find your sister or another way up."

A mechanical sound and a sudden updraft of air caught my attention. The answer I was searching for was in front of me all along. Or rather above me.

"The AC unit," I exclaimed, breaking free from Roland's firm grasp.

"Yeah," he said slowly. "The air turned on. So what?"

"No, you idiot. The AC vents probably lead to the roof, right?"

"Theoretically, they should." He still wasn't following my train of thought but that was alright. I didn't need him to. I knew what I needed to do.

"Lift me up to the vent."

He crouched down and put his arms around my waist. Every inch of my body pressed against his as he slowly lifted me. I stretched my hand up until it touched the ceiling.

"Ok, now just hold me steady no matter what."

Roland let out an agreeable grunt and I closed my eyes to focus all my magic into my hand. I imagined the metal cover of the vent rusting and deteriorating under my touch and as I did, it crumbled into dust around us. The black ink filled my vision and the darkness gripped tighter to the bounds of my sanity.

Roland coughed and shook his head, bringing me back to the moment.

"Warn me next time, would you? My mouth was open."

"You're gonna hate this then," I said as I touched my hands to each side of the vent, rotting away the blown popcorn ceiling a bit at a time until the hole was big enough for me to fit through. "Push me up higher."

"This is as high as I go, Captain."

Without thinking of why or how, I pulled on the blast of air coming from the wide-open vent and sent it under Roland's feet.

"What the," he shouted as he lifted off of the ground. "Avery, dammit. Put me down."

But I was inside the air shaft.

"You can let go," I called down to him. "I'll be right back."

I quit pushing the air under him and heard a thump and his pained muttering as he fell to the floor.

The metal shaft was barely wide enough for my tiny body and I didn't have much room to move even laying on my stomach with my legs and arms outstretched. I nudged myself forward with my fingertips and tiptoes, a little at a time, and manipulated the draft to help me through.

At the junction to the main air shaft, a huge fan blocked my path.

"Just a little more," I whispered to myself. "You've got this."

I sent a blast of dark energy straight at the center of the fan. One hundred years' worth of wear and tear tore through it, and it rusted to a screeching halt. The blades still stood strong though and there wasn't enough room for me to get through.

"*Higher.*"

The whisper was back.

"How?" I cried. "Give me an actual hint."

"*Higher,*" it said again.

I sighed angrily and put my hand on the roof of the air shaft. It started breaking apart. Rust, metal shards, drywall, insulation, and eventually concrete fell to either side of me until light shone through. I slid up into the opening. The roof. At last, I made it to the roof.

I pulled myself up and out of the hole and stood to take in the entirety of the Salem skyline.

FIFTeen

I lowered the hanging ladder I found on the roof to the open window where Roland looked up at me.

"You're going to want to see this!" I yelled down at him.

"I'm good. Really. Just come on down!" he called back.

"Chicken."

"A fear of heights is very logical in this situation," he said as he reached out and grabbed the bottom of the ladder. "If I didn't think you were adorable, there's no way I would be doing this." The ladder pulled taut as he slowly tested his weight on it but it held firm.

Adorable. He thought I was adorable.

There's an ulterior motive. There always is.

His lanky body slid over the lip of the roof, and he sprawled out on his stomach as I waited, tapping my foot.

"Just gonna stay there kissing the ground or are you going to stand up and look at this?"

He slowly lifted his head and then the rest of his body until he was in a sitting position.

"Stand up. You aren't going to die."

"You'll excuse me if I don't believe that coming from a girl that just tried to climb out of a 10th-floor window."

I rolled my eyes and yanked at his elbow.

"Just come look." He shook like a leaf as I pulled him over to the side showed what I needed him to see. "Do you see it too or is it just a me thing again?"

In the distance, surrounded by the only large green patch in view, sat a vivid lavender dome. The rays of the setting sun bounced off of it and sent dazzling patterns into the sky.

"It's got to be the cabin, right?" Roland said, his brain making the connection much faster than mine had. "You guys had that weird magic protection thing over it."

"That's what I was thinking too. What is that place? Some kind of park?" I asked, motioning to the green lush landscape around the sphere.

Roland pulled out his phone. He was an expert googler. He had a result in seconds.

"Salem Woods, or Forest River Conservation Area, depending on the exact location of the cabin. It isn't far. Let's get the car and drive over there." He tucked the phone into his back pocket and headed to the ladder.

"Wait, I have to do something first. I don't want that guy to have to pay to fix everything I broke." I started to summon a small storm cloud full of rain.

"Wait, hold on." Roland took me by the waist and moved me a couple of feet to the right. "There."

"Why?"

"Don't take out the poor dude's Xbox."

I poured rain onto the roof and formed a hole into the apartment.

"There. Now it looks like building maintenance didn't catch a leak that started on the roof in time." Video game slob guy was going to be coming home to a mess, but at least he wouldn't have to pay for it now.

"Oh, better yet." I pushed my fingers gently down on the concrete roof and it crumbled underneath us, dropping us inside the apartment with the rubble.

Roland yelped as his tailbone hit the floor and jumped up to dust himself off.

"Quit doing that," he scolded as he walked out of the door.

I locked it behind us, making it impossible for anyone to tell we were there.

As we descended back down the hill, I bowed in front of the monument, silently thanking whichever ancestors told me to go higher.

The walk back to the car was quicker this time. The careful footsteps of earlier were replaced by excited running. We laughed and taunted each other as we went, barely noticing the growing darkness.

It's another dead end. There's nothing there for you. Don't you realize how pointless all this is?

The New England autumn cold was starting to set in by the time we successfully got into the old grandma wagon. Roland blasted the heat, which was actually colder than the outside air for most of the ride. We turned into a golf range and I could see the top of the violet dome barely sticking out above the trees. But Roland started to turn around instead of going further.

"What are you doing? It's right there." I pointed through the dirty windshield.

"Yes, and so is a locked chain-link fence." He pointed a bit lower, and I slowly dropped my head to see that he was right.

"Seriously, a chain link fence isn't going to stop me if a top floor window didn't."

"So what? We jump it?"

"That's one way," I said, making my fingers spark for emphasis.

"Nope. Nuh-uh. You are not magicing me anymore. I have enough bruises for one day." He shook his head rapidly and leaned as far as he could away from the purple sparks.

You're already hurting him.

"Okay, then we'll do it the boring way and climb over." I got out of the car, laid my jacket across the fence's pointed tips, and climbed to the top of the gate.

Roland inspected it first instead of just jumping over and smugness washed over me. I was so much better at this life of crime stuff than he was.

That's because you don't care if you get caught. No one notices you, whether you're good or bad.

He lifted the arm of the gate, pushed it open with me still on top, and strolled in like he owned the place.

I jumped down, collected my jacket, and didn't say a word, despite how his stupid grin made me want to give him a piece of my mind.

The pendant was going crazy, jumping around on my neck like an excited chihuahua. "Calm down, girls. You're going to choke me out." I laid my hand on top of it and the tendrils of warm, lilac energy twined around my fingers.

Roland smiled and shook his head. "I hope I never get used to stuff like that." He tucked his arms close around himself and shuddered. "Between the spooky woods and the cold, I'm shaking like crazy."

The forest was denser than before and the ground was covered with vines and moss. Moonlight scattered through the branches but never fully reached us. The scuttling sounds of wildlife added to the creepy ambiance of the place.

"Here," I said as I pulled Roland closer to me and pushed the comforting purple magic a little further out. He held back, staring at it as if it would infect him.

He's terrified of you. Of your magic. He'll never be able to accept you as you are.

"It's fine. I promise," I soothed him. "Don't freeze just because you're stubborn."

He leaned back slowly, and our hands brushed. Once. Twice. With every step. And then his pinky was sticking out just enough to catch mine on the next pass. Then finger by finger he moved closer until our hands were intertwined.

He looked down at our hands and grinned. "I hate to say it, but I really like adventuring with you. There's never a dull moment."

"That's one way to say that you're in constant mortal danger when you're with me."

Stupid. Why did you say that? You're so pathetic you can't even properly take a compliment.

I tried to recover. "I mean, thanks. For coming with me. I couldn't have done this alone."

We weren't moving anymore, just two shadows blending into the darkness around us. He came a step closer to me and lifted our joined hands.

Mine was barely solid, my powers taking hold and turning me into little more than mist.

"Does it always do that?" he asked as he lowered his head, and his lips grazed the tops of my knuckles. "When it gets dark. Do you just disappear?"

"I don't know. No one has ever paid enough attention to me to notice." I lowered my head and stared at the forest floor, trying to avoid the awkwardness of looking him in the eyes.

"They're missing out then," he said, kissing up my shadow covered arm to my collarbone. His lips were soft; it felt as if a feather was gently sliding over my heated skin. This is what people meant when they used words like passion, euphoria, bliss. Every cell in my body tingled and longed to hold him closer.

He pulled his lips away from my skin and stared into my eyes. I couldn't move or breathe. The world felt heavy but like it was spinning out of control all at once.

He looked away suddenly and I tried to use the moment to catch my breath. "Do you hear that?" His arms were still around me but his attention was now somewhere far away.

"What?" I asked breathlessly.

"There's bubbling water nearby. Like the creek by the cabin."

The cabin, right. I had momentarily forgotten why we were in the middle of the woods, miles away from home, in the middle of the night.

He started walking, pausing every so often to listen until the woods opened into an all too familiar clearing.

Gone were the fields of herbs and flowers but this was definitely the same place. Roland ran ahead, excited by his findings. Around another bend of trees, he stopped in his tracks.

"Avery, the cabin is gone."

You knew it would be. You knew it was too good to be true.

I caught up with him and stared at the grandiose estate in front of us. A decrepit fountain sat dry in the center of a circular drive and wide ornate stairs led up to a pair of huge carved wooden doors. Vines and other foliage ran in and out of broken stained-glass windows and sections of the wood was peeling off of the sides. The bushes and flowers had escaped their well-manicured basins and spilled out, closing off most of the entryway.

I walked slowly up the stairs, pushing aside years' worth of moss and leaves until I reached the door and knocked.

"Really?" Roland asked. "It's pretty clear that no one is home, Avery."

"It's still polite." My amulet leaped forward, dragging me down until I was level with the doorknob. The pendant hovered in front of it until the gold started to glow with lavender energy and then audibly unlocked with a click.

"Home," a whisper called.

"Hey, the voice is back." I took off the necklace so I could stand up straight.

"Welcome back, disembodied voice that makes us do questionable things," Roland said, smirking.

"Oh, hush. You know you love it," I quipped, putting my hand tentatively on the carved door handle. It opened with no resistance but everything behind it was veiled in darkness.

The moment I crossed the threshold, the house illuminated on its own, revealing a once extravagant entry hall and massive staircase. In the center of the room, an enormous marble statue of a woman stood, covered in flowering vines.

I knew that face. Not from my own memories, but from Anne's. Mary's soft, delicate features looked down at me from eight feet in the air, her hair flowing down past her waist and the carved medallion hanging in its rightful place around her neck.

"She's beautiful." Roland's voice was soft but it still startled me from my reverence. I broke my gaze from the statue and began to explore the rest of the first floor. The stairs were ornate and obviously crafted with meticulous care, but I didn't trust their stability.

One doorway led to an elegant sitting room. With the amount of decay and deterioration, it was clear no one had been here in years. Gold trays sat on a wooden buffet; a china tea set still poised for serving on top. I carefully backed out, strangely worried about disturbing its peaceful ambiance and walked back across the entryway.

Huge oak doors opened into what appeared to be a library. Moonlight drifted in through an opening in the roof and for a moment I was worried it had fallen in, but then my eyes found the small round skylight shining down on a large willow tree. Each wall housed floor to ceiling bookshelves, filled to bursting with books that looked centuries old.

"Avery, come here," Roland called from somewhere nearby.

I found him in one of the long hallways, staring at the paintings lining the walls. Nearly twenty sets of twins, one dark-haired and one light haired but all with a telling upturn to their nose and violet eyes, hung neatly in a row. Decades of fashion were reflected in the paintings as well.

My eyes scanned the portraits and the names engraved on small plaques underneath.

Charlotte and Matilda in full elegant dresses with enough room under their skirts to fit two more women under each one.

Nora and Jessamine in thin silhouette dresses with lace sleeves.

Ethel and Patricia who appeared to have stepped right off the set of Mad Men with cat eyeliner to die for, beehive hairstyles, and high waisted skirts accented by silky blouses.

The last set on the wall was Dawn and Heather, in their twenties like all of the others, but with big teased hair and heavy makeup. Dawn wore leather and had streaks of pink in her black hair while Heather resembled the blonde girl from Charlie's Angels. The similarities and differences between the two would have been comical if my mind had not been doing the math at the same time. If one of these women wasn't my mother, then she was my grandmother.

"For each blessed sister that lives to bearing age, she will be gifted with a son. One of the two sons will birth the next set of blessed sisters," Roland read from a book placed on a podium at the end of the hallway.

I walked over beside him and read the next line aloud. "The new sisters will then come to live with the old, to train and learn, at the time of their twelfth birthday."

Well, there went that tradition. I didn't even know the old sisters, or my own sister for that matter. Come to think of it, twelve was when strange things started happening to me. It was around that time that I accidentally flooded my then foster parent's apartment and the stair railing fell off at another, causing a social worker to fall nearly a full story when she came to take me to my next placement. She was fine. The railing wasn't.

"Above all, the blessing must be concealed from the eyes of the world, lest we face the same fate as Mary," the book went on. I turned to face back down the hallway to the stare and looked at the statue at the entrance.

She had been a lesson to all that came after and her memory was preserved well in this place. She didn't die in vain and her family had not forgotten her. Until, apparently, they did.

There were still so many holes. If either Heather or Dawn was my grandmother, how long had it been since they've been here? Where was my father? Why hadn't he kept me or stayed here?

Who would want you? No one could love someone so cursed and pathetic.

"You alright?" Roland laid his hand on my shoulder.

"Yeah, I'm fine. Why?"

"It's just a lot to take in all at once. I can't imagine it's easy for you."

No one had ever cared about what was easy or not for me. A strange feeling sent a tingle down my spine and the lights flickered. Roland jerked his hand back and looked around worriedly.

"Do that again," I commanded, a theory bubbling in the back of my head.

"Do what?"

"Put your hand on my shoulder or something."

Roland's eyes flicked to my lips and then back up to my eyes and he broke into a sly grin. He lifted one finger and trailed it from my temple, down my jaw, and then ran his fingertip across my bottom lip.

The lights flickered again and Roland's smirk turned into a full, wide- mouth cheesy smile.

"Okay. So now we know the lights are somehow tied to my magic."

"And your magic is tied to me," Roland said smugly.

"Don't let it go to your head. My magic is tied to everyone that pisses me off."

My phone rang and I jumped. I almost dropped it on the stone tiled floor as I scrambled to get it out of my pocket.

"Crap, it's Lynne. We've got to get back." I stuffed the phone back in my pocket without answering it. I didn't have a lie ready about why we weren't home before bedtime. I'd figure it out on the drive home.

"Yeah, Gran is probably waking up about now. She won't notice the car is gone, but she might check on me," Roland said, looking at his phone.

"But now at least I know where this place is. Maybe there's something in here that will help me find my sister. That is, if Lynne doesn't kill me or ground me for the rest of my life."

sixteen

"**Y**oung lady, do you realize what time it is?" Lynne asked from the recliner in the darkened living room the moment I was through the door. I hung my head low, trying to make myself as small as possible.

"I'm sorry. I could give excuses, but I know you don't want to hear them," I said, putting my hands in my pockets and steeling myself against whatever punishment was coming.

"Sit down, Avery." Her tone was unreadable. I looked at the paisley print sofa with its marker stains and scattered throw pillows. Slowly I lowered myself, sitting poised on the edge, ready to run at a moment's notice.

"Before you say anything, I want you to understand that just because I've told you I will not kick you out does not mean I won't punish you. I may not be your birth mother, but you are in my keep. It's my duty to raise you into the young woman you will someday become and keep you safe while doing so."

That was a different twist on a speech I had heard many times before. Never before had someone made me feel so guilty and yet so safe at the same time.

"I'm sorry," I said again, preparing to launch into my practiced lies.

"I want to trust you," she interrupted me. "I do. But you have to be honest with me. No study group ever lasts this long. Avery, please. Tell me the truth. Where were you?"

If I told her the truth, she would have me locked up or sent for psychiatric treatment.

Lie. Lie like your life depends on it. Tell her what she wants to hear.

I knew I should use the alibi I came up with on the way home. But something inside told me she might understand. That she might be able to help me.

She'll never understand you. No one will. She will only think less of you.

I may not be able to tell her everything, but I could get close enough to the truth, so it was believable, rather than my original lie that we had been locked in the library when it closed and had to wait for a janitor to let us out.

"Roland is helping me look for information about my birth family," I said in a burst. Lynne's face fell but her expression told me to continue. "I didn't want to tell you because I don't want to upset you or make you think you're doing anything wrong."

"It's perfectly natural to wonder about your parents. But Avery, you're setting yourself up to get hurt." She shifted around in her chair and her words were slow, calculated.

"Have you gone through this with other fosters? Do you know how hard it is to live your life without knowing who you are?" My voice was desperate, pleading.

"Your biology doesn't determine who you are. Only you can do that. And no. You're my first foster who was old enough to start getting curious. This is a new road for me too." She stood up and walked over to sit next to me on the couch. Her hand reached over as if she was going to pat my knee but she pulled it back.

Disgusted.

"It's strange, Avery. How close I feel to you already. As if you were my own. I find myself wanting to break all the rules they teach us in counseling like hugging you when you're sad and getting used to you being here." She looked down at my knee again. "Stupid things like wanting to put my hand on your knee to comfort you drive me up a wall because I have to second guess my every movement."

"I'm trying to get better at letting people in and not being so scared of touch, but it's hard." I recognized her vulnerability coaxing mine out as well. "Does it scare you that I'm looking for my family?"

She lowered her head. "It doesn't scare me for the reasons you think. I would love for you to find them, because I only want you to be happy. But it terrifies me that you aren't going to like what you find."

"It's like I just came into existence as a fully grown child or something. Can't you see how that would be hard to carry around every day?"

Lynne studied my face carefully, as if contemplating what she should say next. "Do you want to know what's in your file, Avery? It will become public record in a few years. But I think it might be better for you to find out before you age out of the system."

I nodded, not trusting my voice. My emotions and thoughts swirled and shot off in so many directions that I thought the magical energy inside me was going to cause me to spontaneously combust. I needed an outlet for it and quickly.

A door to an upstairs bedroom creaked open. And Lynne sighed. "Let me put Olivia back in bed first. Then we will talk."

As soon as she was gone, I looked out the window behind me at the row of townhouses across the street. A magnolia tree stood between two sets with a concrete bench in front of it.

"I'm sorry," I whispered to the tree as I lifted my hand and brought down a lightning bolt to strike it. It felt like a weight was leaving my body and I could somewhat breathe again.

I laid my head against the back of the sofa and closed my eyes, hoping to clear some of the darkness spinning inside me. Lynne's footsteps descended the stairs slowly and my body went rigid with each thump.

I didn't open my eyes once she sat down beside me, the intensity of her thoughtful gaze too much to bear.

"Before I tell you this, I want you to know I am here. None of this changes anything between us." She gently placed her hand on top of mine. "On your birth certificate, your mother is listed as Jane Doe and your father is unknown. I can't say for sure about your father, but your mother didn't choose to leave you, Avery. She passed away."

I lifted my eyes to Lynne's, fighting the tears that threatened to spill.

"Your mother was found at the entrance to the hospital in the middle of labor. She had no identification on her and died from complications as you were born."

Each word hit me like a blow to the stomach. It was becoming a trend, taking one step forward and two steps back. Finding out information only to have more questions than I started with.

You killed her. If not for you she would still be alive.

"It must be hard to hear that. Is there anything I can do to help? Would you like me to make you some hot chocolate?" Lynne was too nice for her own good but there was no way for her to know exactly how hard it was. She would never know. If the world was kinder, no one would ever have to.

"Is there any mention of a Dawn or a Heather?" I asked, eyes fixed on the wall across from us. I couldn't concentrate too long on the information I didn't have - the dead ends. I had to grasp on to the little bit I did have with my entire being.

Lynne looked confused. "No, hun. No names. Where did that come from?"

I closed my eyes and pressed my thumb and forefinger into them, wishing that, for once, something went smoothly. "Just something I found in the research Roland and I did today. Sisters named Dawn and Heather with purple eyes like mine."

"Oh, sweetie. It's highly unlikely that there is a genetic link because of your eyes." She slid her hand over to pat mine, despite her hesitation, and I leaned my head against her shoulder to show her that I was thankful.

Your hope was useless. You'll never find them.

The sensation of her touch was enough to make the tears breach their borders. Not because I believed her about my eye color; I knew better. But because I had so many questions and so much work to do. I hadn't ever held out hope I would find my mother, but her death was still a jarring discovery.

Lynne put her arms around me and I slid down to put my head in her lap. As the tears kept falling, she ran her fingers through my hair and sang.

"Lullaby, and goodnight, in the skies the stars are bright," she crooned softly. When the song reached the line 'you are your mother's delight' she changed it to 'you are my delight.'

I didn't remember falling asleep or going to my room, but I woke up the next day to the same bright sunlight breaking in through the same window I had woken up to for almost two years. Loud giggles and a series of thumps came from downstairs, making it clear that the Alison and Olivia were up and playing.

I slowly climbed out of bed and went down for breakfast. Lynne smiled at me while she scrambled eggs on the stovetop. She was beautiful, this broken woman with such a large heart. I walked over and laid my head on her shoulder. It was mainly to show her that last night wasn't just a fluke, but also to thank her for understanding as much as she could. She reached up and patted my head with one hand while continuing to scramble the eggs with her other.

Alison gasped from the table behind us. I couldn't blame her; Lynne had told them time and time again that touching me was a no-no. I turned around and sat down next to her at the table, smiling as I did. Her mouth hung open and her eyes were wide, but she didn't say anything.

"Avery, I'm going to run errands today. Is there anything you need while I'm out?" Lynne asked, nonplussed by Ali's reaction.

I thought for a moment before replying. There wasn't anything at the store that could help me find my sister. But it did seem like there would be quite a bit of research in my future. Maybe I could ask for supplies to help without giving it away.

"Is there any way I could get some notebooks? Maybe some pens?" They were benign enough items I knew she wouldn't ask what I needed them for.

"Sure," she answered quickly.

My phone buzzed in my pocket, and I pulled it out to read a text from Roland.

"You in trouble?"

"No, amazingly enough," I texted back.

"Want to catch an Uber to the cabin?"

I looked up at my foster mom, still busy with preparing breakfast. I felt a little bad that I was going to have to lie to her again, but Roland was right. I needed to get back out there.

Lie again. How could she possibly ever understand? She had a family that she pushed away.

"I don't think we can call it a cabin anymore. But yes, ready when you are. But maybe pick me up at the park down the street instead?"

"Oh, devious."

He sees your wickedness.

The moment Lynne and the kids left, I bolted out the door to the park. the Uber was pulling up, Roland already inside, and I jumped in, out of breath from the run.

"Where do we start when we get there?" Roland asked quietly. "Have you figured out a game plan?"

I pulled my backpack around to put it in my lap and clutched it close. "I keep thinking about the library. If there's going to be a way to find my sister, we'll find the answer in there."

Roland looked out the window at the gathering rain clouds. "I didn't get a good look at it last night, but you're probably right. While you're doing that, I'm going to try to get up those stairs without dying."

seventeen

As the rain battered the skylight, I sat under the base of the willow tree that somehow grew in the middle of the library, flipping through a stack of books I pulled off a shelf. I was lucky enough to find an entire shelf of Blessed Sister diaries. Although, once I started reading, it became obvious it wasn't luck that led me to them. It was Anne.

It was always Anne.

Her diary was the first on the shelf, and I couldn't open it fast enough. I needed to know what happened to her, to Ezra, and to the cabin, after I left.

Inside, the inscription read, "To my darling Avery, I am starting this tradition so that one day you may be able to get the answers I couldn't give you before." I held the old leather-bound book to my chest and breathed in the scent of the parchment pages.

I knew Anne would come through for me, I just didn't realize how far she would go to do it.

What good does that do when she's long dead?

My fingers traced the imprint of the ink on the weathered pages and my conscious was whisked away, taking me and every one of my senses back to the cabin I remembered. It was as if I truly had been transported back in time again. Only this time without the dangerous lightning.

I looked around at the cobwebs in the corners and the dust on the floor. Ezra was kneeling before the fireplace, arranging logs into a stack inside it. When he looked up, his face was older, more wrinkled. His eyes crinkled at the edges and when he smiled at something behind me, lines formed around his mouth.

I turned around to find Anne sitting at a desk with a feathered quill and the diary in front of her. Her jet-black hair was pulled into an intricate bun and her dress was more ornate than the one she wore before.

Her voice floated through my mind, though she didn't speak out loud, as she drew the pen across the paper.

"It has now been forty years since that fateful day when we met inside that horrid cell. Ezra and I escaped by the skin of our teeth and traveled under darkness until we were far enough away that the townspeople would not search for us. We settled in a small town in Virginia until the hysteria passed. We only return now to prepare the cabin for its new arrivals, our granddaughters, Judith and Rosemary. I am an old woman now, but I will teach them the ways of the Blessed to protect them from the world and from themselves. I do not know what will happen after that. I have no control beyond my living years, but I will do everything I can to make sure you have a way back to us. Our lost daughter."

A gust of wind and a breath later and I was safely back inside the mansion, still sitting under the large willow. I read on, careful not to touch the ink again. Her story was a roller coaster ride. The escape, relocating, getting married, the birth of their son. Instead of a diary, it read like an old-timey novel. Something out of the pages of Austen or Bronte.

Roland grunted and banged around elsewhere in the mansion as I fell into Anne's transcription of her life. When he tired of fighting with the stairs, he came to sit with me under the tree.

"Well, you can get up them now," he said, out of breath. "But the hallways are blocked off by thorn-covered vines at the top. It'll take another full day at least to clear the entrances." He rested his head against the tree. "Did you find anything interesting?"

"Anne set all of this up for me to find," I said, proud of her effort. "She made each sister keep a detailed diary of their training and lives. Also, Ezra is apparently my however many greats-grandfather."

He let out a mocking gasp. "Shocker."

I rolled my eyes and went back to reading.

"How much longer do you need?" He gestured to the large pile of journals beside me.

"I think I'm going to skip around. I keep looking at the two most recent, but I'm terrified to start them." What if I didn't like what I found? Could I live with whatever those journals held? Could I handle another shock to the system like finding out about my dead mom?

"Isn't knowing, even if it's bad, better than not knowing at all?" Roland had a point. I just didn't want to admit it.

I picked one up one stared at the cover - band names like The Ramones, The Stooges, and The Sex Pistols, carved into it, along with a name in the center. Dawn. Whether she was my grandmother or my aunt, she had good taste in music.

I found myself within the first few pages of her journal, when she was discovering the darkness, confused about how to keep it at bay, worried she couldn't control it, trying to pretend it wasn't there.

But Dawn had a bigger problem.

One she called Bobby Razor.

Bobby was the guitarist in a punk band and her world revolved around him. Before he came around, she was as close to Heather as the rest of the sisters were to each other, maybe even closer. But his distaste for Heather and everything she was about—pop music, peace and unity, and general pacifism—placed a huge wedge between the sisters.

Dawn moved out of the mansion and severed ties with her sister, but she kept her journal. Bobby's attitude got worse and worse, but Dawn didn't see it for what it was. She wrote things like, "I upset him again today. I should have washed the dishes last night like I was supposed to, but I hate doing them when all of his friends are drinking in the kitchen" and "Bobby's friend Thom came over today. He seemed nice enough, but Bobby kept accusing me of flirting, so I stayed in the bedroom alone for the rest of his visit."

I wasn't sure what was sadder, that she went through it or that she couldn't see where it was leading.

As it got more and more intense, I made the mistake of touching the page to follow the words with my finger.

The same blast of cold wind transported me again, this time to a small, rundown apartment. Loud traffic honked and squealed outside. An old folding card table sat in the middle of the kitchen, surrounded by olive green appliances.

He stood in front of me. His bleached spiky hair jutted in every direction, his eyes wild and the veins in his neck bulging.

He was screaming so loudly I couldn't make out the individual words.

I whirled, looking for Dawn. But I was the only other person in the room.

Slowly, terrifyingly slowly, he moved forward and picked up a baseball bat leaning against the wall beside him.

He lunged forward, bringing the bat in an arc headed straight for my head. I threw my hands up to block the blow, but instead the bat shattered into a thousand pieces of wooden shrapnel.

I brought my hands down and stared at them. Was that the darkness? Or was it me?

My eyes slowly drifted to Bobby's crumpled form on the floor. Scarlet red pooled underneath him and I collapsed beside him on the floor, feeling for a pulse but finding nothing.

I rolled him over and found one of the bat's wooden chunks sticking out of his chest.

My own chest was tight, my breathing shallow, the darkness screaming inside of me. Just as I got up to run the cold blast came again, dropping me next to Roland under the tree where I found him sleeping softly beside me like a cat cuddled up for a nap.

Let him sleep. It's his only break from your exhausting personality.

I flipped through the rest of the diary's pages quickly, adrenaline still coursing through me and my hands shaking, but there was very little. She came back to the mansion. She tried to bring Bobby back to life. Her sister followed her back to the apartment and stopped her. After that there was nothing else written. All the remaining pages were blank.

A feeling in the pit of my stomach told me I knew how her story ended, but I wanted confirmation, so I grabbed Heather's diary. I flipped straight to the part where Dawn came home.

The bond the sisters shared was strong and she felt Dawn's pain pour through it. She began to hate their gift, to see it as nothing more than a curse that was stealing her sister from her. She tried spells, potions, wishes on the willow tree, but nothing worked. Her sister faded away in front of her eyes. She spent less and less time out of bed, preferring the peace of sleep to the ever-raging self-hatred and bitterness she felt when she was awake. She talked less too. Never letting Heather know what was on her mind. She became obsessed with trying to find a way to raise Bobby from the dead and when she wasn't sleeping, she was deep in study in the library.

Here.

Where I now sat.

A wet spot formed on the page in front of me and I lifted my hand to find tears covering my cheeks. I had to stop.

I couldn't take any more. Not even if it meant temporarily giving up an opportunity to find more answers.

My eyes burned as I closed the journal. Darkness had descended outside and Roland still slept soundly beside me. I slid out from under the slight weight of his arm which he had thrown over me at some point while I was lost inside Heather's words.

"Dawn, are you here?" I whispered into the empty air. I immediately felt stupid but my amulet lifted off of my neck.

It brought itself to my eye level and its purple glow pulsed softly. I stole a glance back a Roland but he had not stirred.

"You're in there with the others?"

More pulsing. It confirmed my worst fears. This woman I was connecting to on so many levels was dead. She'd let the darkness over take her. Something had gone wrong.

"Are you okay now?"

Pulsing.

"I don't understand."

The amulet flew to the journals and violet wisps of smoke fluttered the pages. It landed on a page in Heather's diary that I had skipped. The amulet hovered above a passage that read, "For once in my life, I am at peace".

"What happened?"

The pages lifted and turned again. This time the amulet highlighted, "Dawn is smart, but she is too in love with love. It makes her do stupid things."

"Love is important, but it's more important to know how to save ourselves," I said, remembering Anne's words, the warning they held.

The amulet hovered over Roland. And if I wasn't mistaken, it was totally judging me.

"Oh." I swallowed hard. "Well. That's not love. He's just helpful."

The amulet pulsed rapidly. Its tendrils of smoke waved around in every direction.

"Okay. Okay. You don't have to yell. I'm focused on finding my sister, not him."

Roland stirred and the pendant fell slowly to the floor, resting on the pages of the open journal.

"Did you say something?" he asked as he opened his eyes.

I picked up the pendant and slipped it over my head. "Yeah. Sorry, just mumbling to myself."

He stood up and stretched his arms to the sky, leaning left and right like a sapling bending in the wind. "We should head back before it starts getting dark. That walk is killer when you can't see where you're going."

I stood and turned in a circle, taking in the vastness of the library and all of its information still waiting to be discovered. "You go on ahead. I'm going to call Lynne and ask her if I can stay the night at a friend's."

"You're really going to stay the night here? As creepy and broken down as it is?"

Creepy. That's what he thinks of you and all you have left of your family.

"It may be creepy to you, but for me, it's everything I need right now. It's the answers to all of my questions. It's the closest I've ever come to a home that's actually my own."

Roland considered this for a moment, and I silently begged the crystal that he wasn't going to fight me on it. Instead, he walked over and put his arms around my waist to hold me close to him.

"If you're sure. I just want you to be safe. Call me if you need me for anything and I'll be here as soon as I can." He kissed my forehead, long and slow.

I laid my head against his chest and heard his heartbeat, steady and rhythmic. We stayed like that for what felt like both forever and not long enough before he squeezed my hand and started to walk away.

He was almost out of the front door before I ran after him. "Roland. Wait."

"Huh?" He turned around with one hand on the door handle.

I ran into his arms and stood on my tiptoes and kissed him, hard. It took him a moment to realize what was happening but when he did, he kissed me back with just as much passion. The lights around us flickered and the ground felt like it was shaking, but that could have been in my head.

He pulled back, looking into my eyes like it was the first time he ever saw me.

"I was, uh, thinking, uh," he started, rubbing the back of his neck with one hand and holding my waist with the other.

"Spit it out, goofball," I said with a laugh.

"So, you know, I know it's not really your scene but homecoming is Saturday. I was thinking we might go. You know, together."

I pulled his head down and kissed him again.

"Is that a yes?" he asked, laughing.

"Duh."

He was still wearing that stupid grin as he walked out of the door and carefully shut it behind him.

Why did you say yes? You know it will be a disaster. You won't know what to do. You'll make a fool of yourself.

I was going to need some extra help to convince my foster mom to let me spend the night away. Strictly speaking, it was against "the rules" for fosters to be in the care of anyone other than government approved caretakers. They even had special "respite care" people in case foster parents needed a break or had to go out of town. And even more complicated, tomorrow was Monday. I had school and should have been home by now to get ready.

Somehow, Anne had compelled Roland to hold on to me when we were transported back to our time. If we could make people do what we wanted them to, I could convince Lynne to let me stay. That charm, or spell, or whatever it was had to be in the library somewhere. But with all the books in the library, I was going to need a spell to even find it.

I stared at the walls and walls of books trying to figure out where to start when a movement on the floor caught my attention.

My amulet started to pulse a soft, glowing light. An idea started to form in the back of my mind, and I lifted the pendant up to my face.

"Is there a spell or charm to make people do what you want?" I whispered to it.

Nothing.

"Oh, come on. You want me to stay here and learn, right? I'll need a bit of help to do that."

Slowly, it started to glow again. The violet energy pulsed out of it like molasses from a tree. I followed its flow to a bookcase at the back of the library and then lifted the book it touched, reading the cover.

The Book of Incantation was imprinted in the white leather binding in a golden, swirling font. Vines of roses bordered the edges. I sat in my reading spot under the tree and read through the different charms.

Spells to lock doors and spells to unlock them. Spells to turn written words invisible, spells to clean dishes, spells to mend dresses. The first few chapters were an arsenal of everyday magic. But it wasn't until I got to the chapter on mental manipulation that I really started paying attention.

Spells to anger. Spells to calm. Spells for love. Spells to make people forget. And then I found it.

A full page on spells to persuade. Only, I didn't know what half of the needed ingredients were, much less how to find them. Before I could ask out loud, my amulet pulled toward a cabinet near the library's entrance. Each drawer was labeled like a card catalog with tiny envelopes lined up inside, each labeled with a strange name like Aconite, Comfrey, or Liverwort. I made quick work of finding what I needed. Balm of Gilead, pink Camellia petals, and ginseng dust. I arranged them in the order the book illustrated and started, badly, chanting the Latin words. I didn't feel any different afterward, but I called Lynne to test it out.

It won't work.

She answered on the second ring. "Avery. Thank goodness you're safe."

"I'm fine," I assured her. "One of the girls from the study group was hoping I could spend the night at her house." Time to see if the spell worked. "It would be awesome if you would let me." I didn't recognize my own voice. It was my mouth, my lips and tongue but a deep, twisted sounding echo came out.

Lynne didn't respond for a few moments. I knew the spell had failed. I started preparing myself to find a bus home.

"I don't know why I'm saying yes, but I'm glad you are making friends."

"Wait, so I can?"

"I guess, but you better get to school on time tomorrow and you don't get to give me any attitude tomorrow because you stayed up all night."

"Thank you," I screamed into the phone, betraying my too-cool, calm exterior.

I was expecting it not to work, to have to rush out and get home as soon as possible. I never thought past this point and had to take stock of my to-do list.

First thing, find a bus route that would get me to school on time.

Second, figure out where to sleep and maybe how to turn off the lights.

Then I would get down to business.

EIGHTeen

R oland's makeshift repair of the stairs held as I walked up to the second level. The main hallway split into two separate wings pointing in opposite directions, but thorny vines blocked both paths. Just like Roland said.

I pressed my hands to the floor and summoned just a bit of destructive energy to the surface. I carefully focused on the vines, not the walls or the floor, in order to prevent a structural collapse.

They wilted away nearly instantly, revealing two pristinely preserved hallways.

I walked down one, looking behind the carved doors at the many bedrooms, sitting rooms, and bathrooms and then wandered down the other. A room that was clearly Dawn's was still decorated in fading gig flyers from punk rock shows and her red-plaid and black bed looked as if it was slept in just the night before.

Life is taunting you with memories of people you will never know.

Out of pure curiosity, I pulled open the closet doors. Inside, black leather and denim hung next to plaid shirts. Her vanity still had Aquanet and makeup on its surface.

I fell in love with her record collection, and to my delight, the old player still worked. I put on Patti Smith's *Horses* album loud enough to hear it through the entire mansion.

Heather's room looked like a crayon box exploded. Her bed was covered in stuffed animals. The walls were covered in posters too but instead of punk bands, they were of celebrities like John Lennon, Shaun Cassidy, and Leif Garrett. A pink and blue plastic corded phone sat off the hook next to her bed.

Between the two bedrooms, Dawn's kept calling me back. There was no way to tell if it was the dark magic, we shared that made me feel so connected to her or our similar personalities but I couldn't deny the growing affection I had for this woman I'd never met.

It was a double-edged sword. If I let myself hope she was my grandmother, and not an aunt, then that meant my grandmother was dead. It had just been a hunch when I called for her in the library and she responded, but it solidified everything I needed to know about how her story turned out.

Yes, that's smart. Get emotionally connected to someone who's dead.

Satisfied with my exploring, I headed back down to the library, Patti Smith's vocals drifting through the halls.

As I slowly worked my way through the shelves, pulling off every book that looked like it might help in some way, I let myself fall into the music. I danced, and sang, and twirled, and spun. The purple smoke of the amulet swirled around me and joined me as I let the music wash the stress away from my body.

Exhausted but excited, I carried the huge stack of books back up to Dawn's room to read them.

There was so much information inside that by midnight my brain felt like it was going to explode. Still no tracking spell for finding my sister.

Frustrated, I looked up to one of the many pictures of Dawn standing with her friends tacked on the wall, directly underneath Sid Vicious' devious grin.

"What was the point of Anne leaving all of this for me if there's nothing here to help me find my sister?" I sighed into the empty room.

A loud crash from downstairs made me jump. I had asked the question with no hope of an answer, but the timing was too perfect for it to be a stray wild animal or gust of wind. Despite my exhaustion, I leapt from the bed and ran to the bottom of the stairs.

The book on the podium Roland read from when we first discovered this place had fallen from its perch and now sat face down on the floor.

I dropped to my knees and poked at the book with my index finger. I don't know what I was expecting, but it didn't do anything.

A bit more confidently, I flipped it over. On the page was a spell for tracking or finding your heart's greatest desire.

Finally.

Even though I searched the entire house, I never once came back to the first book we read. But in hindsight it made sense. If everything else Anne left for me was in plain sight, the one spell she knew I would need would be out in the open too.

You're such an idiot. Running around like a fool when the information was being handed to you.

I read the instructions feverishly and then ran to the library to collect what I needed. Dried strawberry leaves, a jagged piece of amber, white and black candles, and a compass were all inside the card catalog of strange objects in the library.

Despite thinking long and hard about doing it right that second, eventually the need to sleep won out. Exhausted, I packed everything in my backpack and settled in for the night.

At some point in the night, the past infiltrated my dreams. It was too real, too visceral, to be my imagination. Dawn, her eyes black as night, was surrounded by black smoke as Heather tried to fight through it to get to her. The smoke picked Heather up and flung her against a table, knocking her out. Dawn pulled the darkness in long enough to take her own life, ending the threat to Heather's.

When Heather awoke, there was no sadness, no grief, just anger. Heather unleashed all the force of her life-giving magic at once on the mansion and then left. Never to return.

The morning came too soon. I was groggy and it was still dark as I caught the train and while I waited for the next bus from the station. The fight to stay awake continued through the school day and into the evening.

I tried my best not to give an attitude since I promised Lynne that I wouldn't but by the time I climbed into my bottom bunk with my jeans and boots still on, everyone and everything was on my nerves. Even Ali's snoring was driving me mad. The tracking spell would have to wait another day. My heart's desire at the moment was sleep.

Lazy piece of trash.

At last, the moment of reckoning arrived the next afternoon. With Lynne and the girls at soccer practice, I set up the spell on the kitchen table, carefully placing the dried strawberry petals in a circle, lighting the candles, and holding the amethyst over the compass.

I was still crap at pronouncing the Latin words and made a note to myself to download an app to teach myself Latin so I knew what the hell I was saying. But they seemed to work. The compass vibrated in my hand until the needle swung wildly, settling on a direction that most certainly was not north.

I blew out the candles and stuffed everything under the sink out of view of anyone who might come home while I was away and then climbed on my bike. I didn't know how far I was going but hiring an Uber would be awkward when I was being led by a charmed compass. I could only hope my sister was close.

She was closer than I thought because ten minutes later I was standing outside of a grey apartment building trying to get up the courage to go inside.

Just as I was about to go through the front door, it opened and Roland walked out.

When he saw me, his bushy brows knitted together but he smiled.

"Avery, what are you doing here? Did we have plans that I forgot about?"

I shook my head, too stunned to think. He spotted the compass in my hand and gently pulled my hand closer to inspect it.

"Your compass is broken."

"Not broken. Tracking," I managed to say.

"Tracking me?"

I shook my head again.

"I've got to get inside. My sister. She-" I walked around him and opened the door.

He laughed softly. "I would know if someone who looked like you lived in my building, Avery. I'm not incredibly observant, but *that* I wouldn't have missed."

I looked back down at the compass, which was now pointing away from the building and at Roland.

"Dammit," I said as I jumped back on my bike.

"Wait, Avery," Roland called after me. I kept going.

How could you be such a moron? Too busy pretending you could actually do magic. Imposter.

I needed to punch something, or scream, or both. Heart's desire and mildly cute boy-who-annoys-the-crap out-of-you were two very different things. I screwed up the spell somehow. That was the only explanation. Maybe it was because I had been thinking that having Roland's grandmother's car would make things easier. That had to be it.

I would try again tomorrow afternoon. What was one more day when I had waited my whole life for this moment?

It felt like I was floating through life as I tried to pay attention in class the next day, as if my consciousness was somewhere close to my body, but not quite in it. I did notice the signs for homecoming peppered all over the walls and tried to swallow the bile that rose in my stomach from thinking about how much of a disaster it was going to be.

I'd never been one for social functions, but then again, I'd never been given the choice. I could already feel the other students' eyes on me. On Roland. The whispers. The giggles. But I told him I would go, and if nothing else, I'd stand by my word.

As soon as school was dismissed, I did the spell again, this time hiding in the upstairs bathroom that connected our room to Lynne's since everyone was home. Again, the flame of the candles flared and then the compass glowed purple as the needle spun. Again, I followed its lead on my bike.

This time the compass led me to the Medical Center Hospital, a large brick and glass building. It wasn't too far from the house, but far enough that I could believe she might actually be inside. My feet drug as I walked through the main entrance's glass doors. Did I want to know what I was going to find? What if she was sick or injured? Could I handle that?

This is what you deserve. To find your sister and have her ripped away by illness or injury.

I followed the compass until it led me to patient room 436 and lifted my hand to knock. But I put it back down. I couldn't do it. I couldn't go in. It felt like an intrusion of privacy finding her like this.

Thoroughly defeated, I started walking back down the hall. The door clicked open behind me and a nurse walked out, leaving it slightly ajar. Curiosity won out over righteousness. I wouldn't go in, but maybe I could catch a glimpse of her.

You have such weak morals. You can't even stand by your own convictions.

An old woman laid in the bed, her skin, the color of midnight, worn with age. Her white hair was in ringlets around her round face. A boy sat next to her with his head resting on the bed, the brown frizziness of his hair a perfect image of what the old woman's must have once looked like. He raised his head slightly. Sunflowers. Fields of endless sunflowers.

I managed to screw up the spell again. It again led straight to Roland, but I was more focused on the pain on the old woman's face and the hushed, comforting words from the boy beside her. He looked so scared but yet so calm. No wonder he could face all of the strangeness and darkness in my world. He had his own brand in his. My mind drifted back to Saturday when he picked me up in his grandmother's car.

"She's having one of her spells," he had said. Was this what he meant? I knew she was probably the only family he had left. He made that obvious without saying as much. And now he seemed to be losing her too.

I wondered which was worse, having people you loved ripped from you or never having them to begin with. Through all of my restless searching, he was dealing with this but never said a word. He never complained or talked about how he had it worse. He never made it a competition of bad deals.

Selfish. You never once stopped to think about the boy who helped save you over and over again.

Before my tears could fall or Roland could notice me in the hallway, I ran. I ran through the hospital, down the stairs, out of the door. I stopped to catch my breath, or maybe my thoughts, before I jumped back on my bike.

It was all too much. Only one of us could be having a life crisis at once, and it appeared that Roland's couldn't wait. It wasn't fair that good people ended up in bad situations. It wasn't fair that they had to keep going as if nothing was wrong. They had to show up every day smiling and acting normal when their whole world was crashing in on them.

It rained the whole way home and I couldn't help but feel like it was my fault. That my emotions were making a literal dark cloud to follow me around as if I was Eeyore.

I wasn't home longer than an hour when Roland's face popped up on my phone.

"You busy?" his text said.

"Nope. Are you okay?"

"Yeah, why wouldn't I be?"

"No reason. Just polite conversation."

"You're cute when you try to human like a normal person."

I didn't respond. I was too busy grinning like a fool. He texted again. Double texting. Was that a good sign or a bad sign? Possessive or interested? Ugh, relationships were not my forte.

"Want to meet at that park down the street from your house for a few minutes? I feel like I haven't seen you for weeks."

"It's been less than 48 hours, but yeah. I can be there in ten."

The park was dark and abandoned at this time of night. The dim streetlights gleamed off of the plastic and metal playground equipment. The grass was already wet with dew as I sat down on the grassy knoll by the entrance and waited for him.

The lights of the old Buick cut through the fog and created an eerie glow around me. Roland parked the car and came to sit with me. We sat in silence, staring up at the night sky and all its twinkling stars for what felt like forever before he finally spoke.

"It's probably lame. But what are you wearing to homecoming? I want to wear something that will match. My grandmother would get a kick out of that."

When I looked at him, I couldn't help but see the broken boy in the hospital.

"Roland," I started. I needed to tell him what a bad idea it would be to take me to the dance. There were probably a thousand other girls in our school lining up to go with him. With everything going on with me, I couldn't imagine I would be good company and if I was being completely honest, the idea of having to socialize was already exhausting me before the day even arrived.

"I was thinking," he said cutting me off.

I tried again. "Roland."

"We could take my grandmother's car and I'll pick you up around six. I saved up a little so maybe we can get dinner first or something." He wasn't looking at me. His eyes were glued far up in the sky on a single star among the masses. It felt deliberate, his refusal to look at me or let me speak. As if he knew what I was going to say and wanted to change my mind before I could say it.

"Roland, look at me." He slowly turned his full body in my direction. The hope and optimism in his smile broke my heart a bit. "Do you really think this is a good idea?"

"Why wouldn't it be?"

"Roland, I'm— well, I'm me. I'm never going to be someone you can just show off like arm candy."

He gaped at me. "Is that what you think I'm doing? Seriously?"

"I don't know what you're doing." I pushed myself up on my elbows. "I don't know what all of this—" I waved my hand back and forth between us "—is. I'm so close to finding my family and yet here I am, focused on you instead."

"Avery, just because you take time for yourself, or even other people, every once in a while, doesn't mean that you are any less close to finding your family. Don't you ever want to pretend that the big stuff doesn't matter and just breathe for a minute?"

That's what you are to him. A distraction from the negatives in his life. You could be any other girl right now. It's all about convenience.

I closed my eyes and chose my words carefully.

"Some things you can't run from."

His face gradually hardened into stone. "What is that supposed to mean?"

"It means I need to focus on finding my sister and you need to focus on—" I stopped myself before I said too much. "Whatever it is you had going on before I crashed into your life."

"Avery." He put his hand on top of where mine lay on the ground. I pulled mine back away and sat straight up with my arms wrapped around myself.

"No, Roland. Just stop. Stop pretending you give half a crap about what happens to me. Go back to your life and I'll go back to mine." I stood, ready to run, as I ran from everything else, but he stopped me.

"I can't go back now. Don't you see? There's no forgetting you."

His hand reached for mine and a burst of energy shot through my chest and out in his direction, making him stumble back.

He stared at me, mouth wide open and eyes wild. "Did, did you just magic me?"

My face felt flush and my hands vibrated with kinetic energy. I turned and ran, but it felt like running through sand as I put one foot in front of the other. I needed to get away from him. Away from all the emotions he brought that I didn't know how to deal with.

He ran faster though and caught up to me quickly. Grabbing my elbow to spin me around, he tried to catch his breath. "Don't run from this. Please."

Everything went grey. Not completely black. Just gray. A high-pitched scream echoed inside my mind that I couldn't shake. None of my limbs would move. I could see what was happening, but I couldn't stop it as Roland's body flew backward like a ragdoll and he landed in a twisted position on the sidewalk.

No.

No.

No.

This wasn't happening.

This had to be a nightmare.

There wasn't any possible way I would ever hurt Roland. Even if I was angry. This was exactly what I was hoping to avoid by getting away from him. This was exactly what Dawn's story warned me about. I knew he wasn't trying to hurt me. He was only trying to get me to listen. Apparently, either the darkness didn't know he meant me no harm or it chose not to give him the chance.

NINETEEN

The grey started to clear. Feeling returned to my hands and feet and I ran over to his crumpled form, checking the extent of his injuries. Thankfully, it wasn't as bad as it initially seemed. A couple of scrapes and bruises. Maybe a bump to the head. But he was going to survive. His chest rose and fell softly with each breath and his closed eyes fluttered.

I bent over him and sobbed. "I'm sorry. Oh God, Roland. I'm so sorry."

He groaned and opened his eyes slowly. Another round of tears wrenched loose and I collapsed on top of him.

"Hey," he said weakly as he lifted a hand and set it on top of my head. "Aves, stop that. You didn't mean to."

"I could have killed you," I shouted into his now tear stained shirt.

"It wasn't you."

"You don't know that. And if it's the darkness, it's still in my body." I sat up and pulled my knees to my chest, rocking back and forth. "I've got to stay away from you, Roland. At least until I find my sister."

He lifted himself up, wincing as he looked down at his skinned elbow. "Then let's find her."

"Don't you think I've been trying? But every time I do the stupid spell it leads straight to you instead."

His eyebrows shot up. "So, the other day in front of the apartment?"

I lowered my head down between my knees and my chest and avoided his gaze. "Yeah."

"Can I see the spell? I'm not a witch, but the notes in Anne's cabin were pretty straightforward."

My cheeks felt flush as I tried to figure out how to show him the spell without him seeing the title: *Heart's Desire.* How could I explain that one away? "It's more complicated than those."

"Really? How?"

I stammered, buying for time to come up with a lie.

Aren't you good at faking?

The ping of the darkness was exhausting. Its constant whisper in the back of my mind was like an annoying alarm clock.

I decided to fight against it instead. If it wanted me to lie, I'd tell the truth. Darn the consequences.

"It's a heart's desire spell," I admitted without looking up.

If I expected shock or delight, I didn't get it. Just his hand reaching over to take one of mine. "Then we can do it while I'm near you. You can't be looking for me if I'm right there with you, can you?"

I lifted my head and shook it. "You're insane."

"This I knew," he said before he pulled his bottom lip in and bit it between his teeth. "But why this time?"

"For not running away."

195

He raised a shoulder. "You call it insanity; I call it determination. One way or another, we're getting to the happy ending. No matter how hard you fight against it."

I looked at him suspiciously. "Happy ending?"

He rolled his eyes so hard his entire head rolled with them. "You're a perv."

"A match made in prison then," I said with a smirk.

A streetlight above us flickered and Roland looked away from me just long enough to realize how late it was. "You better go. Your mom's going to get anxious."

"She's not my mom," I said.

His head tilted to the side but he didn't push the issue.

"She's my foster mom. My real mom is dead."

Roland screwed up his mouth. "Sometimes the word mom doesn't mean the person who gave birth to you."

The weight of his words told me this was more than an outward observation. We'd never talked about his parents, but the only person he ever talked about taking care of him was Gran. She had to be what he considered his mom.

I blew a black strand of hair out of my eyes. "Yeah, well, Lynne is only temporary. I can't get attached."

He shrugged. "Why not? She is."

"She's kind. Don't mistake that for something more. I don't want to get hurt again."

He smiled as he stood and took my hand to help me up off of the pavement. "Let's get you home. Tomorrow we look for your sister and then the next day we dance."

***

He walked me all the way to the doorway before kissing my hand and heading in the opposite direction.

I walked in and shut the door behind me, leaning back on it as my head spun from the craziness of the night for a few minutes before heading up the stairs.

"Avery, is that you?" Lynne half-whispered, half-shouted from her bedroom.

The house was silent, the other kids asleep. "Yeah," I stage whispered. "Just heading to bed."

She came out of her room, her hair wrapped in a cap and her flowing nightgown draped over her long, lean frame. She looked ghostly in the moonlight filtering through the windows. A single hooked finger motioned in my direction and my shoulders tensed as she headed to the living room.

I followed her silently down the stairs, taking extra care not to step on the boards we knew would squeak. The townhouse was old and my foster sisters slept lightly. There had been so many nights when I first got there when just going to get a glass of water would lead to the entire household waking up. A lot of foster kids were like me. They were on guard all the time. It's hard to feel safe in a strange house. Especially if the reason you are there was because you weren't ever safe in your own home.

In the living room, she motioned for me to sit down while she disappeared into the kitchen. She emerged moments later with a pint of chocolate chip cookie dough ice cream and two spoons. Strictly speaking, we weren't allowed to eat directly out of the carton. Sharing germs was a big no-no. Lynne never restricted our food. That was a horrible idea, especially if you didn't know if a kid had ever gone hungry or been punished by not allowing them to eat. Some foster parents still did it in secret, locks on the fridge and cabinets removed when social workers would come for an evaluation. They said if they didn't, we would eat them out of house and home. That never sat well with me, but I was a kid at their mercy.

Lynne always made sure there was a method to our madness though. We always had to rinse our dishes in the sink and stick them in the dishwasher when we were done. If we took the last of something, we wrote in on a whiteboard on the refrigerator. A drawer of the cabinet was our "anytime" food. Healthy snacks like granola bars and fruit. We were allowed to pilfer that whenever we wanted, whether that was two in the morning or for an afterschool snack. But the stuff high up in the cabinets was for making suppers. To keep so many of us in the same house without drama, there were lots of rules. But lately I was starting to think Lynne made them just so she could break them.

She sat next to me and when she tucked one of her legs under the other and turned her body to me, she reminded me of one of the kids. The look on her face was full of curiosity and wonder. It was the same way Alison looked when she got lost in a good book or when Olivia played a new bubble popper game on the tablet.

This is when she tells you to leave. This is where you lose it all.

"I didn't want to say this in front of the other kids," she started. She was nearly jumping up and down with excitement. Whatever it was, it was big.

Lynne pulled one of my hands toward her and held it between both of hers. "The forms and everything are done. I got all the approvals I need except one. Yours." I tilted my head slightly to the side and stared at her. What on earth was she talking about?

"Avery, it would be my absolute pleasure if you would allow me to adopt you." She paused and eagerly waited for my response, but what was I supposed to say? A thousand thoughts ran through my mind. It felt like a betrayal to the birth family I was looking for, but it also made more sense than anything else ever had. She was already my mom. This would just make it legal. But why did it feel like the end of something rather than the beginning of something else?

"Yes, but on one condition," I pulled myself together enough to say. "I find my sister before I sign the papers." It sounded like a good compromise inside my head, so why did I feel like a jerk once it was out of my mouth?

She looked surprised. "Your sister?" Her body was still, the excited energy that was coming from it now a heavy weight in her shoulders and the corners of her eyes.

"I wasn't the only one born to Jane Doe that night." I sent out a silent prayer that she wouldn't ask too many questions. "I have a twin somewhere. And I can't explain it, but until I find her, I can't get close to anyone. I'll only end up hurting them." What if the next time it wasn't Roland? He was tall, muscular - tough enough to take a couple of swings and keep going. Olivia or Alison would have died in his position. What if the next time I caught Olivia trying to steal my phone because her tablet was dead, or the next time Alison jumped down onto the bottom bunk instead of using the ladder and I exploded on them? I couldn't live with that fear on my head.

"What can I do to help you?" The mother in her was gone, the therapist side fully present.

I smiled as kindly as I could. It wasn't fake this time. I knew she meant well. And I knew that no matter what I said, she would try to help.

"I'm just going to have to do it and hope for the best," I said, squeezing her hand.

"And then once you find her? Are you okay with the adoption?" I could see the smallest hint of tears in her eyes. This was clearly not how she thought this conversation would go. I hated disappointing her, but half-truths would only take us back to square one.

"After I find her. After I know I am not a threat to you and the kids." I desperately hoped she would see that this was to protect them, not because I didn't love her or want to be her child.

She picked up the ice cream container and spoons, filled each of the spoons with a heaping amount, and handed me one. She lifted hers up for a toast like a champagne glass. "Then here's to finding your sister and becoming a family."

***

I'd never been more excited to get out of school and go to a public park in my life. This was it. It was going to happen. I just knew it.

My backpack was filled with the supplies for the spell. Roland had his grandmother's car. Lynne believed I was at a fictional friend's house. All of the puzzle pieces were falling into place.

As I sat down on the grass embankment, I sent Roland a message.

"Ready for an adventure, Roland Bennett?"

His response was nearly immediate. "With you, Avery Smith? Any day."

I was still smiling like an idiot when the old Buick pulled into the parking space in front of me and he motioned for me to get in.

The passenger seat wasn't the ideal place to cast the spell, but it worked and soon, with the charmed compass in one hand and Roland Bennett's smooth caramel hand in the other, we were cruising down the interstate. North. Slightly west. Back to the east. Now back to due north.

This is pointless. You have no idea what you are doing.

My heart fluttered with anticipation the farther we got from home. Logically, we could have needed to travel to Canada or across the country to find my sister, but my heart told me otherwise. We were getting closer. I could feel it in the way the weight fell off my shoulders as we drove. I felt muscles relaxing I never knew I had.

Suddenly, everything was clear. The love in Roland's eyes, the astonishingly vibrant green of the grass that blew past the windows in a blur, the way that the cars around us weaved in and out of traffic like dancers in a ballet when no one knew the moves of the others.

"What do you think she's like?" Roland's voice cut through the sound of the Buick's tires warbling.

"I honestly don't know. I've spent these past few weeks imagining it, but I don't know what to expect. I mean, what if she hates me?"

He took his eyes off the road to send me a questioning look.

"That's not the darkness talking," I said to calm his fears. "It's me. What happens if we meet and can't stand each other?"

"You'll be fine, Avery. She won't hate you. She'll be so shocked to see you she won't know what to think though. So don't push it too far at first."

"Me? Push something too far? I would never," I said defensively.

He kept his head straight ahead and his eyes on the road, but I saw the twitch in his jaw from the laugh he was suppressing.

"Once you find her, what will you do from there?"

"What do you mean?" I asked.

"I mean, are we going to look for your dad or try to figure out what happened at the mansion? And what are you going to do about the multimillion-dollar estate that was handed to you?"

I hadn't ever thought past finding my sister. It was my whole mission. There was no room for anything else like mansions or fathers. Even whatever this was with Roland was on hold until I found her.

"I'll tell you the same thing I told Lynne last night when she asked about adopting me. I just want to get this over with first. We can worry about that the rest later." The needle of the compass swung wildly to the east and then to the south. "Get off at the next exit. I think we just passed it," I yelled out excitedly.

He made his way to the off ramp, navigating carefully past the other cars flying by us. An awkward silence fell until he wasn't weaving in and out of traffic. "Are you at least going to tell me about the adoption thing now that you mentioned it?"

"There's not much to tell," I lied.

"That's crap and you know it," he said with a laugh.

I loved how he saw right through me. Before this adventure I never saw him as anything more than someone who got all the praise that I tried so hard to get. As if his intelligence meant mine was less somehow. Now I was starting to realize that his intelligence meant he was someone on my level. Someone who would understand me without explanation. Someone who I could be real with.

"What do you want me to say?" I asked.

"Well, let's start with the truth. How many foster homes have you been in?"

Go ahead. Scare him away.

I sat completely still in the silence as we waited for the light to turn green.

"Avery, don't shut down. We've come a bit far for that, haven't we?"

He will never be able to love the parts of you that you cannot even love.

More silence.

He let out a long sigh. "Is the compass at least giving us anything?"

"You're headed in the right direction. I'll tell you if it moves."

The light changed and we started moving again. Roland had one hand on the steering wheel and the other holding the top of the gear shift so tightly his knuckles turned white.

"My dad's dead," he said. "Liver failure at an early age. Mom took off shortly after. I see her occasionally when she claims she's clean. She comes in like she's the best mother in the world and doesn't understand why I'm not happy to see her and then she's gone again. You may make tornados, but that woman is one."

I shook my head, trying to understand how we got on this topic. I thought I had made it perfectly clear that gushy stuff made me uncomfortable. "I'm sorry." The sentence was more of a question. An unspoken way of asking why he chose to share that information.

Real smart. Make fun of him for trying to get you to open up.

"Don't be. Gran and Pops have been the best parents I could ever have. I'm just saying we all have our issues." He looked at me and winked. "I'll show you mine if you show me yours."

I laughed and playfully slapped at the arm that wasn't on the steering wheel but then sobered and took a deep breath before I said, "I lost count. But I've been to fourteen schools. They never let me forget that when I register for a new one. And four stays at group homes."

"And you hate that, right?" he asked with kindness in his tone.

"Why would someone like that?"

"I don't know. The adventure maybe? I'm just trying to figure out why you wouldn't let Lynne adopt you if she wanted to." He shot a quick glance my way to gauge my reaction.

"Because I'd like to find my real family."

"And I'd like a sober mom and a dad who's still alive. But at what point do you stop and look around at what you have and decide it's good enough instead of continuing to make yourself miserable?"

The compass swung again and saved me from having to answer him.

"Go back to that street over there. I think we need to turn."

He pulled into a gas station to turn around but instead of getting back on the road, he parked.

"What are you doing?" I asked as he turned off the car and opened the door.

"Snacks."

"Why are you always hungry?" I asked, laughing.

"I'm a growing boy, Avery. Now, do you want something or are you content with feasting your eyes on me?" He was completely out of the car now, his body bent down inside the door frame and one arm resting on top of the door.

I rolled my eyes and climbed out of the car, walking into the store behind him.

He grabbed two long sticks of jerky and threw one in my direction. Holding his out like a sword, he said "En guard" in the worst French accent I had ever heard.

"What is it with you and jerky, man? You eat so much of it you're going to end up one big walking preservative." I put my stick into the air and plunged it toward his.

He hit mine and a battle ensued. "Protein. Dad used to carry packages of sandwich meat in his pockets for snacks. Told me proteins are the building block of the human body," he said between swings and thrusts of his jerky stick.

"Well, I guess he was technically right. DNA is made from proteins. But not that kind," I replied.

"I never said he was a smart man. Thank goodness I got his beauty, not his brains." His dashing smile caught me off guard.

"So, whose brains did you get? Was your mom the smart one?" I had him on the defensive in our sword fight. He was walking backward toward the rows of refrigerated drinks.

"Depends on which side of the family you ask. In my opinion, if either had an ounce of intelligence, maybe they'd still be around." He ran smack into the coolers and I pointed my jerky stick against his chest.

A loud, intentional cough from the cashier had us gathering our purchases and bashfully checking out.

Inside the car, I put on my seatbelt and then asked quietly, "What's it like?"

"What's what like?"

"Having a family. Like cousins and aunts and grandparents and stuff."

"It's like being surrounded by people you don't really like, but love anyway. Like, we get mad and we fight and talk crap about each other. But at the end of the day, we know we have to get over it because we're going to have to deal with each other either way." He didn't move to start the car. Just sat there with his body halfway turned in the driver's seat and his eyes on the crossed hands in my lap.

"It's a blessing and a curse all rolled into one package of people who look sort of like you. To them, I'll never be more than the kid with developmental issues and an obsession with a stuffed bear. Which sucks because they never take me seriously no matter what grades I get or what I overcome. But at the same time, they're the people who will go to bat for me if some crap goes down."

You will never know that feeling. You don't deserve it.

He closed his eyes and laid his head against the seat rest. "At least that's what it was like before Pops died. Now Gran and I are lucky if we see my aunt and cousins on holidays. And I'm not pissed about that for me. I can handle myself. But I am a pissed for her. She deserves the world, and they see her as a burden. Another mess my father left behind for them to take care of."

I guessed that I was supposed to show my scars in return. But there were so many to choose from that I didn't know where to start.

"I caused a dumpster to explode at the group home once."

Roland sat up, looked at me for a moment, and started laughing so hard his body shook.

He's laughing at you.

"There was burning trash falling from the sky like rain," I said. "At the time, I knew enough to figure out it had something to do with me but I didn't know what. I was mortified and went to hide in the bathroom, but the pipes exploded and caused a flood."

His laughter grew even stronger, and he couldn't catch his breath. It was contagious and I found myself joining in despite my embarrassment.

He caught his breath enough to speak. "I love you. You're like 'Oh you've got family problems? I explode crap.'"

"Sometimes literally. Don't let me near a port-o-potty when I'm angry."

There were tears coming out of the corners of his eyes and he wiped them away with his body still shaking in laughter.

"You love me?" Somehow the end of his previous sentence had caused a delay in my computing the first bit.

His laughter quieted. "I mean, I thought that was obvious? I climbed on the roof of an apartment building and took a wicked blow to the chest for you. I wouldn't do that for just anyone."

He can't love you. No one can.

I stared at the propane tank display in front of the car and let what he said process. It had just started to sink in that Roland cared about me, but love was a different story. Love was something I never thought I would know. Was that the feeling that went through me when I got excited every time his name popped up on my phone? Or was it something more? Was it being terrified of losing him or something smaller?

Roland grew uncomfortable and started fidgeting with the keys in the awkward silence.

"I don't really know what love is," I finally answered.

And you never will.

He gave me a smile with only a touch of sadness in it. "I guess we can figure it out together then."

He put the keys in the ignition and pulled out onto the main road.

TWENTY

An ambulance almost took out the side mirror as it raced up the emergency lane beside us. The compass was vibrating so hard it shook my hand. Every nerve in my body sang with kinetic energy. It took all my willpower to stay in the car and try to figure out where we were going instead of jumping out on the side of the road and start running to blow off all the pent-up emotions.

When it swung to the right at the entrance to a hospital, all the excited liveliness drained from my body and was quickly replaced by overwhelming dread. Not this again. I couldn't handle another hospital visit like the last one. This time, I knew it wouldn't be Roland on the other side of the sterile door. It would be her.

The darkness was laughing at me, filling me with its poison.

Roland picked up on my shift in mood. "It doesn't mean she's sick, Avery. Don't worry until we know there is something to worry about." He pulled into the parking lot of the small hospital and parked.

"Take a breath, gather your thoughts, and let's do this. Here," he said, taking the beef jerky from the gas station out of the plastic bag and peeling away the wrapper. "Put this in your stomach, so when you puke with excitement, you'll at least have something to come up."

I took the jerky and tentatively put it to my mouth. I didn't want to eat. My stomach was twisted in knots and thoughts of food were nauseating. But I couldn't remember the last time I ate and Roland was probably right. As much as I hated to admit that.

Staring out of the front windshield, I tried to take a bite.

"No. Don't eat that, you silly goose."

I looked over at Roland in confusion. He had his own jerky stick nearly gone in two bites and was chewing away like a cow on cud.

"Why not? Didn't you just tell me to eat it? Make up your mind."

He stopped chewing and raised his eyebrows at me. "What?" His mouth was full of meat product and the words came out muffled. But the words I had heard were clear and crisp, as if someone sitting right beside me said them.

"Did you not just tell me not to eat it and call me a silly goose?"

He put down his jerky with a pained effort of restraint. I never saw him leave something uneaten when it was right in front of him.

"I don't think I've ever called anyone a silly goose."

We both looked around the car for other people in the parking lot, but there weren't any. We stared at each other for a long time before Roland suddenly opened the car door and rushing around to open mine. "Get out," he said with less command than the words suggested. "Let's do this before you overthink it."

He took my hand and led me down the sidewalk. The compass was hardly any use at this point. The needle swung wildly in circles, like it too was too excited or nervous to function. A chorus of honking noises echoed from the other side of the building and Roland looked down at me. His eyebrows wiggled like jumping, wiry caterpillars

"Geese," he said. "And I'd bet money they are pretty silly."

On the other side of the huge brick building, there was a small pond surrounded by trees and bushes. The loud, pesky geese jumbled around one bench toward the far side of the pond.

On the bench sat a girl, her long blonde hair being whipped and tangled by the strong breeze. She tore pieces off a roll and threw them at the geese as the birds waited impatiently for the next bite.

"Hush now," she said with a voice like a lullaby. "You'll all get fed soon enough. No reason to shout." She swatted at one of them as it tried to bite into the plastic of the bread bag. "I told you not to eat that."

A blue bird sat on her shoulder watching the spectacle. He didn't get scared or fly away when she spoke. Instead, he seemed to be completely at home next to her.

With too many confusing emotions warring in my brain, I tried to yank free from Roland and turn on my heel, ready to head back to the car. But Roland held tightly to my hand and didn't let me pull it loose.

"Avery," he said, drawing out my name until every syllable was its own word. "What are you doing?"

"I can't do this, Roland. Look at her. She's literally perfect. And I'm—" I motioned up and down at my entire body.

"And you," he said, pulling me closer to him and wrapping a hand around my waist, "are also perfect." He bounced his finger off the point of my slightly tilted nose. "But if you walk away now, everything we've been through is pointless. You, silly goose, are a Blessed Sister. You can do this."

The corner of my mouth pulled into a smile and I squished my lips together to try to stop it. "I thought you didn't call people a silly goose."

"Eh, it has a ring to it. What can I say?" He stepped forward, pulling me gently behind him.

I let each footstep drag across the cement and hung my head low.

She didn't look up until Roland was nearly on top of her. And when she did, she must have been surprised to be caught feeding the birds, because she hid the package of rolls behind her back.

Now that we were closer, I could see that her white dress was a volunteer uniform and a funny shaped hat sat beside her on the bench. Of course, she would volunteer at a hospital. I guess you had to do something with all that healing magic. It would have been quite useful these past couple of days.

"Excuse me, I didn't mean to startle you," Roland said as I somewhat hid behind his back. "It's just, I think there is someone you should meet."

I stepped out from behind him, in a bigger reveal than I had planned. I was starting to lose control of my emotions. I was ready to cry, scream, break something, and laugh all at once. A meeting with the sibling who doesn't know you exist would be for normal people to navigate, much less someone like me. Sparks jumped off my fingertips and my hair stood on end with static electricity.

She stood up and jumped back in a motion so fluid that the bird on her shoulder didn't even have time to react. "Who are...?" she started to ask but couldn't quite finish her sentence.

"My name is Avery," I answered, my voice surprisingly steady. "This is Roland." He lifted a hand and gave a tight wave. "I'm your twin sister. I've been looking for you for some time now."

"I don't have any siblings," she responded, her hands clenched tightly to the center of her chest, holding something that glimmered in the sunlight. A cross on a silver and purple rosary. "I'm an only child." The disbelief on her face was evident. She looked at me as if I might disappear if she stared hard enough.

"I'm sorry. I know this is a shock. I didn't mean to upset you. I should go," I said and started to walk away.

"Avery, come back," Roland called after me.

"No, Roland. We tried. Let's just go home." I didn't turn around. There was no point. We weren't going to convince her that her whole life was a lie, even if it was. I couldn't do that to her. She had seemed so happy and content before I scared the living daylights out of her.

And what was with grabbing a rosary and acting like I was some sort of vampire? I missed a good opportunity for a pun there, I guess. 'I don't want to suck your blood, I am your blood.' And then I could have walked away laughing like a Transylvanian castle dweller.

I knew it wouldn't be easy, but it didn't feel like it was supposed to be this hard either. If I knew anything about family from sitcoms and movies, it was that you didn't have to win them over or gain their trust. They were your family from the get-go.

Roland grabbed my arm but I pulled it back again. "No. We're leaving. I can't do this."

He turned away from me and spoke directly to her. "I'm really sorry. This isn't easy on her. I'm Roland." There was a pause in his voice, a question, and she picked up on it.

"Lydia," she stammered. "My name is Lydia."

Her name was beautiful. Just like she was. But I didn't turn around as Roland made more pleasantries and tried to calm her down. I just kept walking.

I hadn't signed up to convince her I was telling the truth about all of this. I couldn't. Because I couldn't even convince myself most days.

Once I was at the car, I tried to fling the door open and get in, but it was locked. So instead, I sat on the trunk and watched the sunset as I waited for Roland to catch up.

"What the hell, Avery?" he asked as he approached. "You find her and then just run away?"

"She thinks I'm evil or lying or something."

"She thinks the whole freaking world is evil. If you'd stuck around, you would have noticed the rosary, and the Bible, and the way she fell to her knees in prayer as I walked away."

I threw my hands in the air. "What the hell am I supposed to do about that? Is that somehow my fault?"

He walked closer to the trunk of the car as the streetlights came on above us. "No, but I'm willing to bet her life hasn't been easy with these powers either. Could you imagine how you would feel if your very existence went against your faith?"

I sighed. "It doesn't. Anne said the gift is a blessing from God. She believed, too. The existence of God and the existence of magic aren't mutually exclusive."

He put one hand on each of my knees and spread them apart so he could move closer to me. "She never met Anne. She doesn't know that."

My head leaned against his chest as he put his arms around me. "I just want to go home, Ro."

"Then let's go home. You've got a dance to get ready for tomorrow."

Twenty-one

"**A**very, are you almost ready?" Lynne asked as she cracked open the door to my room the next evening. Her eyes rolled when she saw me lying on the bed, wearing jeans, an old t-shirt, and worn-out tennis shoes. "Is *that* what you're wearing to the dance?"

I pulled one earbud out. "I'm not going."

She popped out her hip and rested a hand on it. "The hell you're not."

My eyes widened to twice their normal size. "What?"

Lynne couldn't hold the stern facade for long and before I knew it, she was laughing as she sat down on the edge of my bed. "Ms. Keep-my-word Avery is really trying to wiggle her way out of this?" she asked dubiously. "What's wrong? What's keeping you here?"

"I don't have anything to wear. I'm not exactly a 'goes to dances' kind of girl."

She stood up and walked back to the door. "You're whatever kind of girl you want to be, Avery," she said as she left.

I put my earbuds back in and closed my eyes. It didn't matter what cliches she tried to use, at the end of the day, everyone would be happier if I stayed home.

There wasn't a place for me in the real world. Not when I could hurt people. Not when I scared people, even my own flesh and blood.

Lynne bounded back through the door with something hanging over her arm - a sleek black dress with see-through sleeves.

I sat straight up and stared at it. "Where did that come from?"

"I keep an entire closet full of clothes of different sizes." She shrugged. "You never know who is going to come through here and what they'll need."

"I'll look stupid," I said taking the dress from her outstretched hands.

She smiled sweetly. "You'll look beautiful."

I didn't believe her but I shooed her out of the door so I could change anyway. If nothing else, it would be hilarious to see Roland's reaction to me in a dress.

The dress was about one size too big and I nearly gave up again. But Lynne called me into her bedroom, and put one of her belts around it. I had to admit, it didn't look horrible.

"And for the final touch," she said as she pulled out a pair of black stilettos.

I shook my head rapidly. "Nope. Na-uh. Not happening."

"Aw, please?"

"Never."

She put them back in the closet and sat next to me on her bed to brush my hair. "Okay, fine. I'll count my blessings with the dress."

I stared at my reflection in the mirror across from us, or more accurately, I stared at her reflection behind mine. "Do you wish I was more into dresses and frilly stuff?"

Her hand stilled with the brush halfway down my hair. "I don't wish you were anything but you."

We sat in silence as she finished brushing out my hair. She turned me around to face her and pulled a make-up bag from her purse.

"I met my sister yesterday," I said as she slathered moisturizer on my face.

Her mouth formed an O as she stared at me in surprise. "And?" she asked as she regained her composure.

"And she wants nothing to do with me." It would have hurt more if I could feel it. Instead, the darkness took up so much space in my brain that the pain didn't completely penetrate.

"I'm sure it was just a shock for her."

I shook my head. "You should have seen her. It was like looking into a mirror that makes you beautiful, but cruel."

Lynne looked past me to the mirror. "People can be cruel when they don't understand."

The doorbell rang and broke the heavy moment. My heart leaped into my chest.

So excited to destroy everything.

Lynne handed me a tube of ruby red lipstick. "Put that on before you come downstairs. I'll handle your Romeo."

As soon as she was out of the room, I pulled myself off the bed and stared at my reflection. My skin was just dark enough that the black of the dress didn't wash me out and it made the violet of my eyes pop. I hated to admit it, but I looked pretty good. I mean, it could have been worse.

Pretty cocky for someone who's so defective.

I put on the lipstick and walked slowly down the stairs. Roland sat on the living room couch, poised nervously on the very edge of the cushion. He fidgeted with his hands and was chatting with Lynne.

"And you'll have her back before ten, right? Because I will find you if you don't."

I nearly believed the threat, and Roland certainly looked like he did.

"Quit scaring him," I said as I walked down the last few stairs. "Do you want me to go to this thing or not?"

Lynne sighed and waved us off. "Have fun. Just not too much fun."

As the door shut behind us, Roland stopped walking and orbited me. "Dang, Avery."

I looked down at the dress. "Oh, shut up. It's just a dress."

"If you say so."

* * *

Yellow and black, our school colors, were splattered everywhere as if a bumble bee had exploded inside the gym. Our classmates were already in the middle of sweating and grinding against each other to a bass rhythm so heavy it shook the floor.

As soon as we opened the metal doors, I wanted to turn around and run back to the parking lot, but Roland's firm yet gentle grip on my side held me in place.

"You're okay," he leaned down and whispered softly in my ear. "Just stick with me. It will be fine."

I looked up at him and the warmth of his hazel eyes made my knees weak. The flashing strobe lights reflected against his smooth skin. My heart fluttered like a butterfly trapped behind my ribcage. My mouth felt dry, like it was stuffed with cotton. My hands were shaking, but if Roland noticed he was kind enough not to say anything. Instead, he just smiled down at me and led me deeper into the throng of gyrating bodies.

People started to notice our arrival. Several guys turned around and grabbed Roland's shoulder or threw up a hand to say hello, but as soon as they saw me, they turned back around to their dates to whisper. Girls on the sidelines pointed as they giggled.

I held my head low until Roland suddenly stopped in the middle of the gym floor and spun me toward him, pulling me forward into a close embrace. "Dance with me, Avery Smith."

He was an idiot and if he didn't look so good, I'd have told him so. Instead, I let my head fall against his chest as we swayed in the darkness to a Billie Eilish song. Closing my eyes, I breathed in his warm cinnamon scent and felt the tenseness in my shoulders relax.

"Thank you," he whispered against the side of my head.

"For what?" I asked without looking up at him.

"For giving me a chance. For coming to this cheesy dance even though you didn't want to."

I pulled back from him so I could take in his face, to read if the sentiment was genuine or if he was playing with me.

You expect honesty when you can't give it yourself?

"I never said that."

He lifted an eyebrow and I let the words die mid-sentence. It was true that I'd never said as much, but I didn't have to. It was pretty obvious.

The song shifted into another slow tune as the kids around us continued to sway. Roland lifted his hand to tuck a stray strand of my hair back and his thumb lingered, slowly trailing down my jawline until I felt like I was going to explode.

He leaned forward and his lips grazed mine in a tender, almost nonexistent kiss.

Curry, with her horrible timing, locked eyes with me as he pulled his head away. Her high heels clicked louder than the bass beat as she crossed the gym, making a beeline directly for us.

Roland must have heard her or followed my line of sight because he looked back right as she entered the crowd of sweaty, dancing kids.

He looked back at me with mischief in his eyes. "Wanna run again?"

It was the stupidest idea in the book of stupid ideas, but something told me that running from danger with Roland Bennett would always be the highlight of my life.

A grin crept up, unbidden, and he took that as a starting gun. Taking my hand, he jerked me toward the locker rooms. Specifically, the boys' locker room.

It was like watching a car wreck in slow motion. The closer we came to the metal doors marked with temporary pieces of paper that said, 'no entry for dancegoers,' the louder the darkness boomed inside my head.

Look what you've done to him. Brought him down to your level. This won't end well and it's all your fault.

Roland slowed to a stop as the doors shut behind us, sealing us in the pitch-black room. "Now," he said as he glanced around as best he could in the darkness. "Where were we?"

He pulled me closer to him and the affection I'd just started to learn to enjoy made my skin burn with anxiety.

We shouldn't be doing this.

I shouldn't be letting him do this.

He had too much going for him to throw it all away on me.

I pushed him back and slid my hands through my hair. "Roland, we've got to stop. You're going to get in trouble."

His unfailing smile fell slightly but not completely. "I'll be fine, Avery. Can't we just be two kids having fun for five minutes? Do we always have to worry about everything?"

As my eyes closed in frustration, with him and with myself, his hands found purchase on my hips again, pulling me forward as I reached down to remove them.

The door burst open and the multicolored lights from the dance flooded the dark locker room, framing Curry's lanky silhouette like the hero at the end of an action movie.

Her words barely registered as the darkness filled my veins against my will.

"Disappointment."

"Already given a warning."

"No choice."

"Expelled."

The floor started to vibrate and crack. The lockers around us opened and slammed shut over and over again. A bitter cold descended, making each breath a cloud of smoke as the lights flickered on and off.

Roland tried to get my attention, but he was a blur against the grey filling my vision.

Something snapped, a wet, sick sound and I came to enough to see Curry trapped between two locker room doors. They'd closed with no consideration for the body between them. Her eyes were closed and my heart dropped into my stomach.

I couldn't have killed her. What would happen to me if I had? Suddenly, I wasn't as worried about expulsion as I was about a jail cell.

Roland was beside her before I could bring my legs to move. He turned around to look at me, as if he knew the thoughts running through my brain. "She's still alive. I think she just took a blow to the head. Help me get her out of here."

He pulled at the doors, but they wouldn't give.

With a flick of my hand, the doors opened, and Curry lurched forward onto Roland's shoulder. He lowered her to the ground with care.

Taking advantage of him being occupied, I bolted. He called out behind me, but I didn't stop.

With tears streaming down my face, I pushed through the crowd and out of the gym doors. And then I kept running. Down the street. Blocks away from the high school, stopping only when I thought I was far enough that Roland couldn't have followed.

I reached into the corner of my bra where my cellphone was tucked because of the lack of pockets in the godforsaken dress and pulled it out to call Lynne to pick me up.

She didn't ask questions as I climbed into the white minivan with mascara running down my face and my hands still shaking. She didn't ask questions as she walked me into the house and tucked me into my bed. She didn't ask questions as she kissed my forehead and shut the door behind her.

And, somehow, that solidified my decision. These people were too good. I couldn't put them in any more danger. I needed to leave so their lives could continue the way they should. I was a burden, a burden that would eventually rot them from the inside out.

The only way to relieve the infection was to remove the destructive body.

An image flashed into my mind. A rumpled, onion skin thin piece of parchment with scrawling handwritten notes. A title at the top: "Forgetting Spell."

I pulled my phone out and flipped past the thousand pictures of Roland, memes, and class notes. All the way back. To pictures too old for my phone to register the date. To the snaps Roland took of the notes in Anne's cottage. Among the many, the one I needed was waiting clear and crisp, as if it knew I'd be back for it.

"Tomorrow," I told myself. "I'll do it tomorrow." Tonight, would be my last night in this warm bed. My last night pretending I was someone worthy of a calm, stable home.

TWENTY-TWO

S leep took me into a numb surrender until the light broke through my uncovered window. I sat up, pulled on clean clothes, and stuffed my backpack full of supplies.

By some miracle I already had everything I needed for the spell. Which was good because everything in my arsenal was back at the mansion, and I was going to need this spell in order to get there. I gathered some strands of their hair from their brushes, moon water from a plastic bottle in my windowsill that I forgot to throw away, a hunk of black tourmaline I stowed away in my backpack, and a white candle. Lynne's vanilla bean crème candle would have to work.

I started chanting before I even opened my bedroom door. I repeated the spell over and over again as I walked through the small townhouse. I made eye contact with each of my foster siblings. Olivia downstairs on the couch, tapping at some reading game on the tablet. Alison, her red curls sprawled out across the side of Lynne's bed, her lanky legs up against the wall as she held a book up over her head. The words didn't want to form on my lips. Two years of this soft, quiet, sweet girl sleeping right above me. She would forget every moment. Washed from her memory as if I never existed.

But I had to do it. They were safer that way. They needed me to protect them. From me.

The smell of the hair burning in the candle must have alerted Lynne, because I walked down the stairs to find her blocking the front door. Her arms were crossed as if she were a bouncer preventing me from leaving. Her mouth was a straight line, and she swung her head back and forth, her microbraids making a rustling noise as they knocked each other around.

"Whatever you think you're doing right now, Avery, you're not in a good state of mind to be going out on your own."

I kept chanting. Kept walking forward. When I closed the space between us, I put my hand on her shoulder and looked into her chestnut eyes until they unfocused. Her body went slack for a moment, and I made my escape, knowing I had just erased all memories of myself from the closest thing I would ever have to a mother.

Outside the front door, I fell to my knees and wretched. My stomach did somersaults, and my ribs ached. My hands shook as I pulled myself up to peer into the front bay window. No one ran after me. I could only hope that the spell worked and life continued as normal for them. And it would keep doing so. As long as I never showed up here again.

★★★

I couldn't ride my bike the entire way to Salem, so I had to leave it at the train station and hopped on the red line. I would miss it, but it was just another casualty in the long line from today.

You can't run from yourself.

Once I made it to the mansion, I couldn't bring myself to study in the library as I should have. I couldn't worry about learning how to control my powers. I couldn't bring myself to do anything except lay in Dawn's bed and cry until my entire body felt empty. My eyes burned, my nose ran, and the back of my throat ached. To top it all off, I had somehow given myself a headache with the sobbing. I couldn't even muster the strength to pull the plaid duvet up from the bottom corner of the bed. Completely void of all thought and emotion, I stared at the wall. Not the posters. Not the pictures. Just a blank space of white paint. My breaths went in. My breaths went out. I was still living, but I might as well not have been.

Purple vapors poured from the amulet and down my body until they reached the covers that I was too lazy to grab and pulled them over me. A small gift from my ancestors, I guessed. Not that it did me much good. The ice inside me wouldn't be thawed with a warm blanket.

I don't remember falling asleep, but soon the light of the sun pushed its way through the black curtains and illuminated the spot on the wall where my eyes had been glued. My stomach growled. I had to pee. My muscles ached to move. My arm was numb from the position I was laying in. Biology was winning over my reluctant mind.

I shuffled into the bathroom. Thank the crystal for magical plumbing. I walked past the mirror and didn't recognize myself. My hair was forming knots and tangles and the bags under my eyes were almost as purple as my irises. What fifteen-year-old has bags under their eyes? My skin was pale, too pale, as if I was as dead as I felt.

The shower taunted me with its pristine tile, untouched for years but still glistening. I couldn't remember the last time I truly felt clean. I didn't think I could ever scrub enough, get the water hot enough, or the soap strong enough for me to wash away the grit and grime. It was a kind of dirty that felt like it had always been there, somewhere under the surface.

Even if I could bring myself to go through the motions, it wouldn't do any good. I was exhausted. The thought of standing that long or expending the energy to wash my hair and body felt like a monumental task.

I climbed back in bed without brushing my hair or teeth and stared at the wall some more. When the sun was high outside the window, I checked my phone for the first time that day. I didn't expect anything from Lynne, but it still felt like a dagger to the heart when there weren't any missed calls or messages from her.

Scrolling through the junk alerts proved pointless. A Youtuber posted a new video, I could claim three gems on a game, a coupon for ten percent off at Target, and other useless information. Nothing felt right. I had no interest in doing anything. Watching a movie sounded boring, all my games seemed futile, even listening to music had lost its appeal.

With all the effort I could muster, I drug my feet down the stairs to the library and started reading through the titles on magic. 'Chaos and Genesis' was written in Latin, so that was a no go. 'Shadow Travel and Other Forms of Astral Projection' showed me some neat little tricks to turn into a shadow to move around quickly or visit places without moving my physical body. 'The Darkness Inside' sounded hopeful, but it was all about reading other people's minds and their dark thoughts.

I pulled out the 'Book of Sacred Writ', the book that used to be on the pillar near the stairs. I had already gone over this book time and time again but something inside me told me to read it one more time. So I cracked open the old leather binding and read every word on every page.

Halfway through, I stumbled upon a page that I could have sworn wasn't there before.

Children of Night.

I turned the page to make sure. The next was Children of Light. Well, it was clear which I twin was. Nothing about me was light. I was definitely the dark twin.

Evil twin.

"Those with the power to harness the dark also hold the powers of chaos, destruction, and decay. These sisters tend to have a hard time reconciling their powers with their good nature," it read. Good nature. Yeah, right. Obviously, the author had no idea what this family lineage would dissolve in to.

"Decay, in its true form, is the gift of life from the old to the new. It is a transformative power meant to shelter and promote growth." Okay, I could give the book's author that one. I had watched Anne crumble leaves into fertilizer for the sunflowers.

"Destruction is similar. Tearing down the old makes way for the new in the constant circle of life. This power, when used correctly, can transform trees into wood for shelter or fire or chip away at stone to create tools or sculptures." I felt like this was pushing it. Destruction was, by definition, the opposite of helpful.

"The darkness is not the absence of light as most think. The darkness is the calm in the race of life. It is required by all living things. It's the respite in the commotion of existence. It is a lullaby to the cacophony we exist in." I almost put the book down. This was pro-darkness propaganda if there were such a thing. Did the darkness write this? Because it kind of sounded like the darkness wrote this.

I closed my eyes, took a deep breath, and started reading again despite my frustration. "The darkness should not be confused with so-called 'black magic' or 'low magic.' There is no demonic or wicked nature to any of the abilities of the blessed sisters. Their magic comes from nature and its energy." Not demonic. That was a good thing at least.

"A child of the night divines their powers from the moon, the stars, and the shadows. The practices of Astrology, Geomancy, Alchemy, and Telepathy fall within the realm of darkness." I could totally get behind the ability to read minds. And alchemy? The only thing I knew about it was that old guys used to use it to turn random things into gold.

Did that mean I could turn things to gold? Hello, new bank account.

"One must always live with restraint as both the Light and the Dark can be harmful to their vessel. Moderation in the amount of magical energy expended is the only way to avoid the potentially disastrous consequences. The symptoms of reaching one's limit can be deceptive. Intrusive thoughts, immense sadness, and lethargy are common. But less obvious signs include a reluctance to feel emotions, apathy, and confusion." Check, check, check. This was a lot to take in. It was one thing to know that there was a limit and something entirely different to know that I had been riding so close to it for so long.

"Children of the Night must listen to their bodies and their souls. They must take active measures to protect their mental state. These may include rest, sensory pleasures, or forms of expression that lessens the burden. If they push themselves beyond their boundaries, they should fully cease their magical activity until all symptoms subside." That wasn't an option. Now that I was on my own, I needed my powers to survive. The food in my backpack and the twenty-seven dollars in my pocket were only going to go so far.

I would start small, dabble in alchemy maybe, and then work my way up to more complicated stuff. Surely, I would have more indication if the darkness was getting too close. Yeah, there had been some warning signs, but there was no way it was bad enough that I needed to stop yet. If I saw I was pushing myself too far, I would stop. Simple as that.

I pulled more books off the shelves and got to work. The harder I trained, the more in control I felt. It took nearly a week but soon I could move things around the library with my magic just as easily as flicking a finger. I turned several leaves from the willow tree into gold and others into crystal and ruby just for fun. I used the shadows to travel from the library to Dawn's room to get a granola bar out of my backpack and then back downstairs. I found a really neat spell and turned my hair different colors before settling on purple. Because, well, it fit my aesthetic.

The magic kept coming easier and easier. It was like I tapped into a reserve I never knew I had. I felt powerful for the first time in my life. Nothing up to this point mattered anymore. The circumstances of my birth, my time in the foster care system, my sister's hatred for me. Because I was reborn the moment I learned to unlock my magic. This was what I was made for.

I pushed my ability to shadow travel further and further. First to the woods outside and back. Then to the street. Then to the Target to use that ten percent off coupon and the last of my cash to get some more food. I was going to have to find a way to turn those gems into cash. I was pretty sure Target wouldn't accept golden leaves. All of the magic was making me super hungry. No matter how much I ate, I didn't feel full. The hunger gnawed at my stomach and made me nauseous, but when my adrenaline was spiking, I barely noticed.

It was a rush, almost addictive, to be able to do whatever I wanted whenever I wanted to do it. I could breathe easily for the first time in my life. I missed my family for once I didn't have to worry about any of those trivial things like what people thought about me or if someone somewhere was disappointed in me yet again.

Anne was wrong. A life not shared with others was freedom, not just the passing of time. I was free from prying eyes, free from rules, free from judgment. The only thing that would make it better would be having my sister here. If I could somehow convince Lydia I was safe and not remotely evil, I could set her free too. We could live in the mansion away from the rest of the world, together without any strife.

When I got back to the house from Target, a message from Roland chimed on my phone.

"I smoothed everything over with Curry. She doesn't remember a thing, but we need to talk."

I didn't respond. I should have wiped his memory too, but I was more worried about getting away before I could hurt him or anyone else even more than I already had.

The text pushed me to a decision I was already leaning toward. I had debated finding a spell to change Lydia's mind about me. To somehow show her what we could be together.

It was time to do it.

It was time to be with my sister.

TwenTy-THree

According to the books, not only could I learn to read minds, but I could also do it from a distance. If I really wanted to test my limits, I could influence the thoughts within those minds. Essentially, I could search for her mind with my own, using her power to draw mine to her like a magnet and then twist it to my whim. It would take more magic than I had ever used before and undoubtedly push me to my limit. It was scary and exhilarating all at the same time.

I wished I could have tried it on a smaller scale first. Read someone's mind who was in the room maybe, or only a few miles away. But there wasn't anyone nearby and I didn't want to take the time to shadow travel and find someone. I just wanted it done. I was tired of waiting. Tired of training. Tired of doing things exactly as they were supposed to be done. I was ready to jump into the deep end and hope to the crystal I could swim.

I put my phone on my Spotify playlist, figured out how to adjust the lights, and lit scented candles all around me. Throw pillows from the bedrooms upstairs covered the floor. The setting was as peaceful and serene as I could make it.

I read the instructions one more time, just to make sure I hadn't missed something. I couldn't screw this up like I screwed everything else up. It wasn't the time for my bad luck to strike. I needed my sister. She would be the only one that would understand me. She would be the only thing that could stop these evil thoughts from taking over my mind.

It was just like a recipe. Or so I told myself. Just add the right ingredients in the specified amounts. Follow the directions. Don't deviate.

I closed my eyes.

I chanted the Latin words in my head.

I held the necessary stones inside one clenched fist, my amulet in the other.

Somewhere in the blackness of my mind, blue lines intersected and branched off from each other over and over again. They shot out in all directions like a spider's web, growing and forming and shifting. Thoughts filled my mind. Thoughts that were not my own.

"Now, what did I do with those keys?" a man's voice echoed.

"He could have at least let the dog out," a woman's voice broke in.

A sensation of falling forward without moving washed over me. I lost touch with reality. There was no longer a floor beneath me or a ceiling above me. The music slowly faded until I was surrounded by a heavy silence. The smell of jasmine and vanilla from the candles disappeared. It wasn't cold. It wasn't hot. I swirled and twisted and lost shape as

I floated through the strangers' thoughts, searching for the one I needed in the crowd.

I was nothing. No body. No emotions.

Just a single thought.

Find her.

In the distance, all the blue lines converged on a single bright star. Its glow illuminated the dark corner of my mind. With a feeling I couldn't describe but couldn't ignore, I knew it was her. The star started to morph and take the form of a girl's silhouette. Long hair billowed out into the darkness like blue petals on the wind.

I mentally pushed myself harder. She was just in reach. Just a little farther.

Vines made of a black gooey substance appeared and crept up the blue lines, deteriorating every centimeter they touched. Suddenly every bridge to my sister was crumbling before me as if the blackness was acid. I started to spin wildly out of control. With no body, there was no way to know what direction was right side up, but the sensation spun my insides like a cotton candy machine.

No.

This couldn't be happening.

The darkness was catching up with me at the worst time possible. I tried to scream but had no mouth. I tried to open my eyes in my physical body but I couldn't. There was nothing I could do but watch as the blackness edged its way toward me. Soon it was crawling into my vision, engulfing everything in some shade darker than black.

Once it was finished, the fear was gone. But so was everything else. I floated inside the blackness with no memory of why or how. Everything was washed away. No longer was I worried about getting to my sister or if Roland and Lynne were going to be okay. What was the point? I could just stay here and exist in this blackness forever. No one would notice. No one would care. Life would continue on without me. It wasn't like I had ever made an impact on someone's life or ever made a real connection. I was one of many. A background player used to make the movie feel more real, but without any story of their own.

There was a sound in the distance. A voice. A whisper. Familiar, but I couldn't place who it belonged to. Memories pulled at the back of my brain but I couldn't quite touch them. Like they were on the other side of a heavy curtain.

"Avery," the whisper called.

I am a small child in the back of a stranger's car. I don't know where I'm going. I barely know where I came from.

A field of green and yellow outside the window as we speed past. I open the door of the moving car and step out into the field.

A breeze plays with the hem of my shirt.

I reach out to touch one of the flowers blooming far above my head. But it grows taller, just out of my reach.

I stand on my tippy toes. It grows taller.

I grab the stalk and bend it down, but the moment my hand meets it the flower disappears, replaced by a boy with caramel skin and frizzy hair.

My hands are no longer around the stem of the flower.

They are around his neck.

I am no longer bending the bloom down to my level.

I am bending him backward.

I am hurting him.

I snapped back to some semblance of reality. The silhouette of a human body was visible just beyond a thick cover of black smoke. It wasn't my hand around Roland's neck, but tendrils of shadow twisting and curling around him like a snake.

I couldn't move, couldn't stop it. The darkness enveloped him. His face contorted in anguish. His fingers clawed at his throat. The black smoke's grip lifted him into the air. His legs kicked wildly, trying to gain purchase on the surrounding furniture. Paralyzed, I was glued to the scene in front of me. I couldn't look away from his pain. Higher and higher the smoke lifted him until his body went limp and dangled in the air, a sickening reminder of the statues of the hung accused witches at the wax museum.

The smoke let go and his body started to drop from the twenty-foot height he'd been suspended at like a heavy stone.

A lilac glow broke through the smoke. At first a flicker, then a flame, then a raging inferno.

The shape of a woman appeared within the fire.

Purple vapors swirled and shifted, moving this way and that, but there was clearly a woman ascending to catch Roland. Surrounding him in purple tendrils, the woman lowered him to the ground. A glint of light at her feet caught my eye. The woman was standing on my amulet.

When the darkness took over, the amulet must have slipped from my grasp. That was the only way to explain how it escaped the sphere of darkness that held me prisoner.

Upon closer inspection, she wasn't standing on it. She was coming from inside it.

With Roland safe, a war of purple and black smoke erupted in front of me. Flashes of light like tesla coils and black clouds filled the room. The ethereal silhouette turned slightly as she waved her hands to control the flurry of lightning. In profile, a sliver of her face appeared. Dawn's face. Dawn had come to save me from the darkness.

On the other side of the battle, Roland came back to consciousness. He sat up, confused at first but coming to terms with the epic battle in front of him with impressive speed. He looked for an opening between the lightning and the looming darkness. He was trying to get to me. When he found a break, he rolled under the blackness and barely dodged another attack. Another violet figure appeared from the ether of the amulet. An older, more distinguished shadowy woman with her hair up in a grey braid atop her head. Anne, in all the withered beauty old age brought her after I left, distracted the fluid-like tendrils as Roland turned around to motion someone else through the onslaught. Who else would have come for me? Who in my life would care enough to put their life in danger?

As soon as I saw the dark braids piled on top of her head, my questions were answered. She was clearly confused beyond measure. I didn't know what Roland told her to get her here, but it couldn't have been enough to justify the scene playing out in front of her. I could only hope that in the midst of the chaos Dawn or Anne had given her the permission she needed to see the mansion.

The pair ran to me, skirting around the edges of the fight. Roland reached up and grabbed one of my feet and Lynne grabbed the other. I was suspended in midair, level with the bottom branches of the willow tree.

I couldn't tell who was winning and had no feeling in the rest of my body. Though now that they touched me, I could at least see that I had a body again. They yanked me down to the floor and Lynne enveloped me in her arms. She shook with sobs. She repeated my name over and over again. Roland stooped beside her, a worried look in his eyes. I laid limply across her lap like a ragdoll. Even though I was in control of my own thoughts now, I couldn't move. I was trapped in my own mind. I was powerless to tell her I was alright or reach out and hug her back.

The darkness gradually retreated back in to me as if I were a sponge soaking up spilled black ink. With their battle over, Dawn and Anne turned to face me. Anne's hand reached out and closed around Dawn's as they smiled at me.

I yearned to be able to reach out and touch them, to hold them. To thank them. But I was still paralyzed, and the helplessness ate at me.

Looking around the room, I savored a view I never had the pleasure of before. Each person, or person-like apparition, inside these four walls was someone who loved me. Loved me enough to set aside their own problems and focus on mine for a moment. They loved me enough to stand in the line of fire to save me.

Lynne, with her unfailing sweetness, gave a home to a child no one else wanted. Roland, in his stubbornness, refused to give up on me. Anne and Dawn had guided me and loved me even without me knowing. I was too blind to see it before, but I could see it clearly now. This was my family.

"You've never been truly alone," Anne's spirit whispered as it turned into a swirling funnel and burrowed down into the amulet, disappearing from view.

Before I saw her silhouette catch Roland in midair, the concept of blessed sisters inside my amulet felt hokey. How many times had I spoken to it and felt like an idiot? How many times had I thought I would never get it back during a move or a stay at a group home and it appeared the moment things calmed down?

Seeing them appear was something else to get used to. I owed my life to my ancestors, to Dawn and Anne, in so many ways that were just beginning to occur to me.

Twenty-four

R oland reached over to grab the necklace and slipped it over my head. A burning sensation washed through me as the last of the darkness was dissolved by the crystal's amplification of my power.

Testing my control of my body, I lifted my hand. It was solid and moving on my command.

I sat up and looked back and forth between Roland and Lynne.

"How?" I asked. My throat felt like it was coated in sandpaper and the words came out as a hoarse croak.

"How did we know to come? Or how did I get your mom? Or what?" Roland unhelpfully asked.

I squinted at him. "All of it."

"Well, when you didn't respond to my message, I got worried. And, well." His hands motioned around us and he raised his eyebrows. "All this has been going on. I thought it must be related."

"Sorry about that." I twisted my mouth sideways.

"At first, I figured you didn't want to talk because you like to do that whole dark, broody thing. But after a while, I started thinking the worst. When I came to the house and your mom had no clue who you were, I knew something was wrong."

Lynne raised her hand to stop him. "Let's not give the girl an anxiety attack right now. There will be time to explain later. For now, you go find her some water. She sounds half-dead."

Roland, the good boy that he was, left and headed to the kitchen.

Lynne pushed a lock of my hair behind my ear. "I get it," she said softly. "I get why you felt like you couldn't say anything, but it doesn't change the fact that you didn't have to go through all of this alone. I may not be your mom—"

"But you are," I stopped her. "You're the closest thing I've ever had to a mom."

She wiped at one of her eyes with her shirt sleeve. "Oh, sweetie. You really know how to make an old woman cry. Just like I told you the other night, I will be around as long as feasibly possible. And I might not always understand, but I can promise to try."

I didn't deserve her. Darkness or not, I had done nothing that warranted the amount of patience and love this woman had for me. If there was a blessing in my life, it wasn't my magic. It was this woman.

"I tried to save you from all of this," I said quietly. I had failed. Instead of protecting her, I brought her into all of my craziness instead. "I thought if you couldn't remember me, you wouldn't be in danger."

She laughed softly. "You aren't as good at your spells as you thought. The moment Roland showed me your picture, everything came rushing back."

"I didn't know Roland had a picture of me."

"You're all over his phone, baby girl. He's a good boy. And cute, too." Her crooked smile told me she knew Roland was more than just a friend.

"Lynne!"

"What? I've got eyes. I knew the first moment he showed up on our doorstep that he had it bad for you."

"It's not like that."

She raised her eyebrows and we laughed, because we both were more than aware it was, in fact, just like that.

Roland walked back in with a china teacup full of water.

"You look better," he said as he sat down next to us and handed me the cup.

"I feel better."

He settled more comfortably on the ground next to me as Lynne scooted over to give us more room. "Do you want to talk about it?"

Their watchful eyes were kind, but I could tell they wanted something from me. I expected the darkness to buck against the tightening in my chest. To tell me to hold everything close, lest they think I was insane. But, to my surprise, it was quiet. There wasn't even a whisper.

"I was so freaked out. Lydia hating me. Worrying about disappointing Lynne." I glanced over at her half-smile. "Not being able to control the darkness. Turning you into some kind of juvenile delinquent when your gran needs you to be there for her. All of it was too much." I stopped suddenly. I knew I had said too much. My eyes widened as I looked at the shock on Roland's face.

"What do you mean by that?" He didn't sound angry, just confused. He deserved an explanation even if it hurt. If I had learned anything, it was that being open and honest was better than being secretive for the sake of protecting the people I cared about.

"The tracking spell didn't just lead me to your apartment. I saw you with Gran at the hospital." I hung my head. I couldn't meet his eyes.

He lowered his own head and tried to make me look at him. "She isn't well. She hasn't been well for a long time, Avery. We deal with it. Every once in a while, she has to go in and get the fluid drained from her lungs. But she's better for a bit after that." He lifted my head and I brought my eyes to his. "You just saw her on a bad day. She would be embarrassed, but I'm not. She's a strong woman. I'm proud of her for that."

"I didn't want you to have to worry about my stuff when you had your own to worry about," I said.

"That's what being friends is about. I'll help you with your stuff because I care about you and one day, if I need it, you'll help me with mine. That's what it's like to have people, Avery."

I now knew I had people. Real people. People that gave a crap.

Lynne hugged me a little too tight. "I'm going to give you two some time to talk. I have a mansion to explore," she said as she got up and walked out of the library, a look of amazement on her face.

"I tried to find her again," I said after a heavy moment of silence. "Well, not just find her. I tried to find her mind, and change it about me. It didn't work."

He looked down at me and took in my worried expression. His face was so soft, so bright. It was such a contrast to the drama we were still going through.

"So how do we fix it? What can I do?"

"I don't know. The book said I have to rest before I can do more magic. But even with that, I'm scared. I don't know if I can delve into that world again until I absolutely have to. And I can't change her mind without it."

"Well, if rest is what the princess requires." He stood and scooped me up. "Rest is what the princess will get."

I unabashedly squealed with laughter as he tried to carry me up the stairs and failed miserably. "The princess requests to be put down now, please."

"Oh, thank God," he said as he put me down. "I was trying to be extra but you're a lot more solid than you look."

"Hey," I said as I shot him a glare. "Dark matter has more mass is all."

Once I was settled in Dawn's bed, Roland walked around the room, picking up album covers and looking at the pictures on the walls. "Your aunt was hot," he said as he pulled out a picture tucked inside the edge of the mirror. "She kinda looks like you."

"Her name is Dawn and she totally saved your butt earlier."

"Yeah, I wasn't even going to ask about that. Apparently strange purple ghost ladies are where I draw the line," he laughed.

"I'm just glad to know there is a line. I was starting to think you might be even more insane than I am. I mean, who else would be cool with their girlfriend going all black smoke monster from Lost and not say a word?"

He sat on the edge of the bed beside me. "Girlfriend, huh?"

"Don't gloat. It isn't cute on you," I said as my lips betrayed me and involuntarily twitched into a grin.

"But obviously something about me is. Because I can't imagine that the enigmatic Avery Smith would date someone who isn't cute." He leaned forward and brought his lips to mine. Fireworks exploded inside my mind. My nerves tingled with an excited energy. I brought my hands up and knotted my fingers into his hair, pulling him closer. He rolled forward, laying me down on my back as he held himself above me with his elbows.

A cough from the doorway made us sit up and jerk apart.

"I'm gonna give you this one because it's been one hell of a day," Lynne said as she walked in. "This place is huge. There's a lot more to it than you can see from outside. There's a ton of rooms I couldn't get to because of some overgrown foliage."

Once I found Dawn and Heather's rooms I stopped exploring. For all I knew an entire family lived in one of the blocked off wings.

"I've always wondered what it would be like to live somewhere like this," she finished.

The hint of an idea crossed my mind and my eyes shifted back and forth while I debated how it would work.

"You know, we could always move you and the kids in here."

I'd never seen someone's head jerk around so fast. "Avery, don't even joke about that. You know I couldn't accept that kind of charity."

"But it wouldn't be charity. As much as the townhouse feels like home, so does this place. If I could combine the two, I'd be set. And can you imagine how excited the kids would be to each have their own room?"

Her eyes squinted as she thought about the possibilities. "You know you're one of those kids, right? And that would take a lot of money. Think about the electricity bill for this place. And the furniture we would need to replace. And the money for movers and boxes. I can't come up with that kind of money from nowhere."

"I can, or well, I did. I can turn certain rocks into other rocks. Like rocks that are worth money. I made some gold and rubies before the darkness caught up with me."

Roland and Lynne shared a look that I didn't quite understand.

"Avery," Roland started. "The darkness is you. We've known this from day one. Anne made it very clear. It's not a separate thing trying to harm you, it's your own mind."

Lynne put her hand on top of mine. "I've seen this before in kids with depression. They turn their negative thoughts into some kind of monster that exists outside of themselves. Figuratively, of course. It's hard for someone to wrap their mind around their own brain fighting them. Granted, your case is a bit different since your magic does literally turn into a separate being, but I think we can treat it the same way."

"Is this where you tell me you're sending me to the looney bin or putting me on a cocktail of medication?"

Her eyebrows lowered into that look she gave one of us when we smarted off.

"Neither of those are things to be ashamed of. They both help people. But some cases don't require that level of treatment. I think some counseling and self-care activities could go a long way."

I rolled my eyes and Roland snorted.

"Avery isn't big on self-care."

"Obviously. But look where that gets her," Lynne responded.

"Guys, I can still hear you," I said as they laughed.

Now that everything was in the open, I knew things would change, but there was some illogically hopeful part of me that hoped they would change for the better. That *wanted* them to change for the better.

TWeNTY-FIVe

I laid in my bottom bunk and listened to Alison's now comforting snoring. Things had started getting back to normal or as close to normal as possible in the weeks following the battle at the mansion. Days were filled with school, which thankfully I hadn't been expelled from after Curry lost her memory, and nights with Lynne and the kids.

My downtime now included a Lynne-imposed hobby to keep my mind occupied, although I got to pick which one. I was getting pretty good at picking away on her late husband's acoustic guitar.

Roland became hellbent on making me relax. On the days when Lynne said it was okay, he would come over after school and do stupid things like clean my room or read to me out of one of our textbooks to help me study. When he was there, I never had to get my own plate of supper or glass of water. He ran himself ragged to make sure I was okay. I wished I could say it wasn't helping. I hated being waited on hand and foot. I wanted so badly to fight it on my own and say I would be okay. It was a punch to my pride to need people like this.

But it was helping. I hadn't heard the darkness again since that night. The ever-present swell of emotion in my chest grew lighter. My head quit feeling quite so full. Breaths came easy and the constant fatigue left.

Still, I was scared to use my magic again. The memories of the nothingness haunted me. Nightmares racked my body at night- the black ooze, the feeling of falling forever, the sight of Roland's body breaking under my touch.

And without Lydia, it felt like there was a huge piece of me missing. Like feeling pain in a limb long after it was removed. I needed to somehow convince her to give me a chance. It was the only way to keep the darkness at bay long enough for me to learn how to control it.

Roland and Lynne couldn't continue to treat me like a porcelain doll who could break at any moment. I could see how much their worry and concern were wearing them down. And Roland needed to focus on his grandmother. I felt like a fraud because she really was sick and everything that was wrong with me was all in my head.

He assured me that what I was going through was just as valid, just as harmful, and that Gran was doing better. Or so he said. But I wasn't sure I believed him. Even with the dark thoughts subsiding for the moment, I couldn't help but feel like Roland told me what I wanted to hear.

It would have been easy for me to tell myself that all of the negative thoughts were just the darkness taunting me, but in reality, even the happiest people sometimes had a hard time being unfailingly positive. I had to come to terms with the fact that I wasn't going to get better overnight. It was going to be a constant battle and fighting it every moment was the only way to keep winning. I had to be more self-aware than ever and remind myself how I perceived the world wouldn't always be how it really is.

My brain often lied to me. And it wasn't just the lies of the darkness trying to make itself more powerful, but my perspective of the world around me lied to me. My view was cloudy with perceived anger or hate, when there was none there. This was my reality. Even having Lydia around might not change everything. The darkness still took Dawn, even with Heather, her counterbalance.

My phone pinged on the bedside table, and I smiled, knowing it would be Roland saying good morning and asking to stop by after Gran's treatment.

I rolled over and clumsily grabbed the phone to tell him it would be fine, but when I unlocked the screen, I saw it was an Instagram alert.

I'd made my account forever ago but only used it to follow bands I liked. There were a few pictures stray black cats, a shot of me in my favorite leather jacket that Lynne bought me shortly after my arrival here, and one of my hair after Alison put purple hair chalk in it. Sure, it had my name on it, but no one from school, not even Roland, had followed me.

'CoalByTheCross' had sent a single message. "Is this really you or am I annoying the wrong person?"

I wasn't sure what they were asking, and the profile picture was too small to determine if I actually knew them so I pulled up the account.

As soon as I did my heart skipped a beat. It was Lydia. Her blonde hair flowed like a wheat field in the breeze in every picture. Flowery skirts, a green house, and multiple pink drinks clogged the feed. Apparently, she had a cat, one of those freaky hairless pointy ones, named Ruth. Ruth appeared to have more jewelry and outfits than I did. There were pictures of mission trips, her arms around orphan children in various parts of the world. There were pictures of the beach in all seasons, as if it was her go to place.

I held my breath as I responded. "It's me."

Only two words, but so much rode on them.

It wasn't long before my phone buzzed again. "I have questions."

I bet. I could have answered them, could have helped her come to terms with everything, if she hadn't run me off. Or maybe I ran myself off. Maybe it wasn't her fault I couldn't deal with her fear.

"I may have some answers. Do you want to meet up?"

There was no reply. Sick with anticipation and nerves, I got up, slipped a cardigan over my tank top and sleep shorts, and padded downstairs for breakfast.

I jumped so violently that I spilled the orange juice I was pouring when the phone vibrated again.

"Not yet. I'm still coming to terms with the whole being adopted thing. Seeing you was like a smack in the face."

She immediately followed up with, "No offense though."

I couldn't relate, of course, but I wasn't offended. No one ever told me I was biologically theirs. No one ever pretended for me. I knew from the moment I could comprehend my circumstances that I was alone. "None taken. I know it's a lot."

"What are we?"

That was a loaded question if I'd ever heard one. "We are Blessed Sisters. We've been granted the ability to manipulate nature." Maybe if I kept it basic enough, clean enough, she wouldn't freak out and run away again.

"By who? The devil?"

I closed my eyes and took a heavy breath as I reached for a paper towel and tried to slop up the spilled orange juice. "No. Our ancestors believed it came directly from the universe, from whatever God or deity runs that mess. This would be a lot easier to explain in person."

"I don't know why I'm telling you this. But I'm scared. I can't control it anymore. And there's this voice in my head. I think I'm going insane. If you can help me, then I'll meet you. I don't want to live like this anymore."

The glass cup slipped from my fingers and shattered at my feet. I thought that the darkness was only limited to the Child of Night, that the Child of Light was immune to it. Was Lydia going through the same thing I was? Was the darkness haunting her, too?

I needed to get back to the estate, back to the Book of Sacred Writ, and read the page about the Light. Otherwise, I wouldn't have any answers for her.

But, first, I needed to clean up even more orange juice and shards of glass before one of the girls slipped or cut their feet. As I did, I sent a message to Lydia with the mansion's address.

"Trust me, you'll want to meet me there. I think I can help, that we can help each other."

With the burden of hiding myself from the world lifted from me, I had no reason to lie to Lynne anymore. I poked my head inside her bedroom to tell her I'd be going to Salem today. Olivia slept curled at the foot of her bed like a sleeping cat, but Lynne was wide awake, propped up on the headboard reading yet another book on child psychology.

"My sister is going to meet me there."

Her face lit up and then quickly hardened to a worried expression. "Do you want me to go with you?" she whispered.

I shook my head. "I'll be okay."

"At least take Roland with you. You need back up."

"This isn't a police raid." But I knew she was right. I'd be lying if I said I hadn't thought about it too.

Plus, Ubers to Salem were expensive and I was broke, now that Roland and Lynne wouldn't let me cash in the precious stones I had made. His grandmother had officially given him the Buick last week on his birthday in a massively understated version of a sweet sixteen. The three of us, plus Lynne and the girls, ate at a Mexican restaurant and then Gran threw him the keys and said, "Drive me home in your new car?"

It definitely made things easier to have a boyfriend with wheels. Especially when I was splitting my time between a foster home and the real-life Barbie Dream House my dead family left me.

Another thing that made things easier: a boyfriend who actually responded to my texts. After a few taps, he was outside waiting with the understood caveat that I would supply the chicken nuggets.

***

I waited by the front door of the mansion, impatiently pacing around the statue of Mary. It felt like the statue was waiting too, but I knew that was just my imagination. I checked out the window approximately every five seconds for her to arrive.

I wasn't nervous about whether or not she would be able to find it. She was a Blessed Sister; she was born with the ability to see it. I just wanted to see the look on her face when she did. It's not every day you get to show someone a mansion filled with their bloodline's history. It was a special moment and I wanted to savor it, but it felt like it was taking forever for her to get here.

"Come in here and stop pacing," Roland said from the library.

"I can't help it," I grumbled. "Shouldn't she have been here by now?"

"She'll get here when she gets here. Manchester isn't just around the corner, you know."

"I know. I know." I stomped my foot like a child. "I'm just not good at waiting."

Roland sighed and kept looking through the book he had pulled off the shelf.

I sat down next to him under the willow tree and had an idea. I looked over at him and double checked that he was lost in study mode before I closed my eyes and let my mind drift through the thoughts around me. I tried to stay away from Roland's even though they were pretty loud. It felt like an invasion of some sort of privacy code. I looked for Lydia. Her face, her voice, her thoughts. Now that I knew what I was looking for, it was easier to ignore the other chattering and the blue lines that led off in the wrong direction. Her mind called to me.

"She's out of the Uber and walking this way," I said, jumping up and going back to the door.

"You did not just read her mind because you don't have any patience," Roland said, rolling his eyes but putting his book down and following me to the door.

Lydia emerged from the tree line, and I ran out to meet her. I stopped short of throwing my arms around her and hugging her. We weren't there yet, but I had to believe we would get there one day. With time. Right now, it was my job to ease her into the water I'd been thrown into and not scare her away.

"Welcome to the Blessed Estate," I called out to her with a sweep of my arm to indicate the grand house behind me.

"How long have you been sitting on that one?" Roland asked quietly.

"Just came to me," I responded out of the corner of my mouth.

"Bull."

"It's definitely something," Lydia responded, staring at the huge staircase and lavish beveled windows. "This is ours?"

"Yep, it's been in our family since it was just a one room shed really. According to the records, it was torn down and rebuilt in the eighteen hundreds."

"Hey, I happened to like the shed," Roland chided me.

Lydia widened her eyes and tilted her head. Her eyes darted between me and Roland and the mansion.

I smiled the most innocent smile I could muster. "That's a long story. Why don't you come in and look around?"

Inside, she stared at the statue of Mary with her mouth hanging slack. I knew what she was seeing. The same thing I did when I first saw the wax figure on the field trip. Her mirror image.

Her eyes dropped to the plaque at Mary's feet, and she read her name out loud. "Mother Mary. How ironic."

I tilted my head back and forth. "More like super great Aunt Mary, but I see where you're going."

She fought back a grin. "Have you always lived here? Do you know our parents?"

I pretended to be removing a scuff on the tile with my boot instead of looking at her. "No. I—"

Roland's arm slipped around my waist and gave me strength. I looked up at him and his lips lifted into a smile.

"I just found out about all of this, too. I've been in the foster system until now." The unsigned adoption papers inside my backpack crossed my mind. I'd left them there, waiting until it felt right. Waiting until I could reconcile this makeshift family I'd quilted together with the one my DNA gave me.

"So where are they?" She was walking in circles around the statue, reaching up to trace the carved vines and flowers swirling around Mary's dress and hair.

"That's kind of a big question," I said as I looped my fingers around Roland's and squeezed. "My birth certificate said our mom passed away. No dad listed."

A purple spark at the tips of her fingers was the only sign she was distressed. A mask of calm indifference colored every inch of her features.

She looked down at her hands where the sparks continued to flow. "I guess now is as good a time as any to ask about this," she said as she held the hand up.

For fifteen years we had dealt with this alone. It would be hard recovering from the scars that would leave, but now she was asking for my help for the first time.

"I don't even know where to begin so bear with me, please?"

She nodded subtly and I gestured for her to follow me to the library where the Sacred Book of Writ sat open by the tree's base.

Before I grew too impatient to sit still, I'd skimmed the pages about her type of magic. It seemed in the Blessed world, no one was spared from the downsides to their powers.

She followed my lead and sat beside me.

"Lydia, I know you're scared. I know that the voice in your head is making you feel anxious all of the time, like something bad is going to happen at any moment. I know it tells you that you have to be perfect in order to not let other people down. But it's wrong. It's your powers messing with your head."

I opened the book to the page she needed to see and pointed at it. "Mine are similar, only instead of lying to make me anxious, it fills my head with dark thoughts that bring me down. If you lean into it too much, it will consume you."

She read as I talked and I quieted to give her some time to take it all in. Going back in time and almost being hung for witchcraft wasn't an ideal way to discover my powers but this wasn't either.

Roland busied himself in another part of the mansion. We had started to renovate, or as best two teens could, to make it feel more like a home. Thankfully, I was able to reverse the effects of our grandmother's magic with my own for the most part, although some things would take actual construction workers to fix, like the leaky roof.

For now, strategically placed pots and pans would work.

I still hadn't claimed a bedroom, and Lynne didn't feel comfortable enough to let me stay here by myself at night so there were no more sleepovers in Aunt Dawn's room. But on the weekend, Roland and I made this place home during the day. It was our refuge. And hopefully, it would be Lydia's as well.

Her eyes darted from the page to the violet veins in her hands, then her leg which had been bobbing up and down ever since we sat down. "How do I stop it?"

I gave her a knowing smile and leaned forward to close the distance between us and take her hand in mine. I wanted to show a bit of affection, let her know she wasn't alone.

But instead, a strong gust of wind nearly knocked us flat on our backs the moment we touched. A black cloud rose from my body as white steam lifted from hers. Above us, the two swirled together into a grey mass of air.

It separated and combined over and over again, the black mixing with the white and then, just as quickly as it left our bodies, it split into halves and returned.

We stared at each other with wide eyes before Lydia found her breath to speak. "Is that normal for you?"

"Nope," I responded as I shook my head and reached for her hand again. "But let's find out if it's supposed to be."

No clouds appeared but an electric sizzle covered my body with goosebumps. I gasped and looked over at her. An immense weight had been lifted off my chest. I could breathe like I never could before. My mind felt clearer than ever.

She looked back down at her hands and up at me. "It's gone. Is that all it took?"

"I don't think it's gone forever, but I think it will be easier to fight it together."

Together. It was a word I was saying a lot nowadays. To Lynne, to Roland and now to Lydia.

"So, this," she said as she laid her hands on either side of the willow tree as the crystal connected to her rosary glowed so bright, I could see it through the pocket of her bleached jeans. The tangles of branches expanded in all directions, growing under her touch. "Is this because of my blessing?"

I lifted my own hands and waved them, trimming the tree down to its normal size. "Yes, and this is my blessing." The words felt weird. It was the first time I said them out loud.

The first time I let myself admit that my powers might be something more than just a curse. "Just as you can control the powers of light and creation, I can control darkness and destruction."

She shrunk back. Maybe those weren't the right words to use with Lydia. I tried again. "I just mean you are one side of the circle of life, and I am the other. Our powers complete each other."

"This all sounds so demonic." The judgement was back but it didn't seem to be solely directed at me this time. It was quickly becoming clear that she was just as scared of herself as she was of me and what we were capable of.

"No. You can relax. There is nothing demonic or wicked about our powers. They come from nature, that crystal inside your rosary, and our emotions."

"Our emotions?"

I was starting to wonder if she only spoke in questions. She sounded like a parrot.

"I know it sounds weird. I'm still trying to figure out some of it myself."

She slowly lowered herself down onto the throw pillows. "How much do you know about me?" she asked quietly.

"I know that whoever you think are your parents aren't your real parents. I know you're fifteen and your birthday is June 18th. I know about the time you turned twelve weird things started happening to you that you couldn't control or explain. I know that animals listen when you talk and other people's emotions overwhelm you."

She stared at me; her expression frozen in shock. Maybe I shouldn't have told her everything I learned from the Sacred Book at once. A slow introduction into all of our weirdness probably would have been best.

Lydia's phone rang and she pulled it out of her back pocket. The rainbow unicorn case caught me off guard. I mean, yeah, she was bubbly. But that was a case better suited for Olivia's tablet than a fifteen-year-old girl's phone.

"Fire trucks," she muttered under her breath.

"Excuse me?"

"It's my mom. She thinks I'm at Bible study."

My brows knitted together. "I used the 'study group' excuse myself when I was researching all of this. But what does that have to do with fire trucks?"

"Oh, it's just something I say instead of cursing," she explained as her cheeks flushed with color.

"Okay, then. Anything I can do to help with your mom? Want me to sing Jesus chants in the background or something?"

She cracked a slight smile but waved off the suggestion. "I hate lying to her, but she has no idea about any of this."

Me.

She meant her mother had no idea about me.

Which wasn't my battle to fight.

And even if it was, there wasn't much I could do about it.

As kindly as I could make my voice sound, I said, "Ask her for some more time. I'm not ready to give you back yet."

Tears welled in her eyes as she sat motionless and stared at me. I knew that look- it was a look of pain being healed. I didn't know what she'd been through, or why me wanting to be near her mattered so much to her. But I knew it did. And that was enough for me.

TWENTY-SIX

It was nearly a month before we saw Lydia again, but I talked to her nearly every day. Snapchat, Twitter, texts, every form of communication available. Except Facebook. Her parents, for some reason, monitored her Facebook like hawks.

I didn't expect to have a relationship with her overnight, but we were from such different worlds.

Her and her overly religious parents and wealthy life, and me and the scraps of a family I sewed together. It wasn't so much that I was jealous. I knew what I had was important. I knew that her life was less glamorous than it looked on the surface. But I couldn't see how we had any similarities to draw on.

There were no self-help books for establishing a relationship with your counterbalance when you've spent a decade and a half apart. I was navigating this blindly and hoping for the best.

She did research on our parents on her own, but always came up empty handed.

Until one day she didn't.

Until one day I got a message that changed everything.

"The last tax deed for the land the estate is on is registered to Heather Garner."

It was followed by a string of emojis that I could only assume would have been a string of expletives in someone else's hands.

Pretty soon my phone was blowing up with pictures of our grandmother. Her husband. Her obituary.

Her son.

Our father.

"Meet me at the mansion?" she asked as soon as the last picture came in. "We have work to do."

Roland and I did more research as we waited for her to arrive. Heather's son, Oliver, looked like a grown-up version of Ezra, all Chris Pratt-y and beefed up.

"He has a Wikipedia page, Avery," Roland said as I clicked back and forth on ancestry sites.

"Give me that," I said, yanking his phone out of his hand. "Are you serious?"

"I don't play about Wiki pages."

An American technology entrepreneur, investor, and engineer.

Founder and CEO of Dreamland Software, a company that produces machines that can wake you from nightmares or supposedly send you into dreamlike states.

I felt Lydia's presence before she walked in the door and I knew that if I let my shields down, I could have heard her thoughts as she approached.

She burst in the door without bothering to knock, which was appropriate because she had as much claim to this place as I did.

"I assume you've been looking him up, too."

"He's a freaking billionaire," Roland said with absolutely no couth.

Lydia blanched but didn't scold him.

I sat quiet, unsure how I felt about the revelation. Unsure how I felt about having a father who had been alive this whole time. All I could think about were the still unsigned adoption papers. About how Lynne's face would look when I told her I had a dad.

"So, what do we do with this, Aves?" Lydia asked as she came to sit beside me in the redone parlor.

"I don't know." It was the best answer I could give her. It was the best answer I could give myself.

She took my hand in hers as I stared off into the distance. "We don't *have* to do anything with it. You know? We have each other now."

Roland, standing opposite of us, smiled at the sentiment. "Yeah, Avery, we've all got each other now. You don't have to do any of this by yourself."

I picked up my phone and continued to flick through pictures of Oliver leading models down red carpets, cutting ribbons at restaurants, speaking in front of crowds. The man lived the life of Bruce Wayne without the vigilante secret identity, at least that I knew of. But then again, I just found out he even existed.

I clicked the side button to lock the phone and closed my eyes, even though Oliver's image was now burned into my eyelids, so it did no good. I didn't feel like crying, but I didn't feel like cheering. It was a strange feeling of shock. Finding my dad felt more like the icing on top than the cake. It was an unexpected surprise.

Lydia's hand moved from its place in mine to my shoulder. "Look, I'm not good with not knowing things. It's part of that whole feeling anxious thing, I think. But now we know. And we can leave it alone if you want to. I guess I just went a bit mad with curiosity."

Her presence was calming, like a favorite teddy bear calms a child or the perfect song makes everything feel better. "

That's why I'm here, I guess," I said after a moment. "I'll be the calm to your crazy if you'll be the day to my night."

For the first time in my life, I actually felt like everything was going to be okay. That tomorrow, or the next day, or however long it took before the darkness reared its ugly head, I could defeat it. It didn't have its vice grip around my heart and mind anymore.

It didn't matter if we went to find our dad or not. I had everything I ever needed now.

Roland, Lynne, the kids, Lydia. Each one was a wedge driving the darkness farther away and helping me learn how to fight it for myself. We may have been a misfit group and it may have taken me fifteen years to find them, but I knew in that moment that I wouldn't trade my newfound family for anything.

273

"Come back to the townhouse with me, Lydia. Please? I want you to meet some people."

She pulled out her phone and checked the time. "I told my parents I was training to be a camp counselor so they don't expect me back for a little while."

***

I let her ride in the passenger seat of the Buick because I wouldn't wish the cluttered, French fry smelling, chocolate-stained back seat on anyone. As Roland drove, we talked about everything under the sun, except our dad.

Out of the corner of my eye, my backpack kept catching my attention on the floorboard beside me.

It was time. It was past time, if I was being honest with myself.

I picked it up and unzipped it, pulling out the papers and laying them across my lap.

"Ro, do you have a pen in here?"

He looked at me from the rearview mirror. "Are you doing what I think you're doing?"

I felt my cheeks grow warm as I nodded.

Roland looked over at Lydia with a huge smile. "Quick, before she changes her mind. There should be a pen in the glove compartment behind the napkins."

Lydia looked confused but didn't hesitate to dig through the tiny space in front of her and came up with a single, chewed up ball point pen.

I took it from her and pressed it to the paper.

"What's going on?" she whispered to Roland.

"She's signing the adoption papers."

Lydia was still confused but smiling. We'd talked a lot over texts, but my damage was still too much to talk about at times. She had no idea how huge this was, but she was willing to cheer me on anyway because she could tell it made me happy.

"That's a good thing, right?"

"It's a great thing," Roland responded as he pulled into a parking space in front of the townhouse. "You'll find out why in just a minute."

There was no fanfare. No one threw confetti. No one alerted the media.

But the look on Lynne's face as I slid the papers in front of her on the table was better than all of that combined.

She was crying before she could even get out of the chair to wrap her arms around me. "Oh, baby," she muttered over and over as she violently swayed us back and forth. "My baby."

It wasn't long before she noticed the extra person standing beside her. She straightened but didn't let go of me while she used her shoulder to dry her tears.

Lydia smiled sweetly when she saw she'd caught Lynne's attention. "It's a pleasure to meet you, Avery's mom."

Lynne, in true Lynne fashion, reached out and pulled her close with her free hand while still holding me tight with the other. "Oh, silly girl. Come over here. You're family too." Her head craned over the two of us. "Roland Bennett, if you don't get your butt over here and join in on this hug, I'm gonna tell Gran."

He snapped to attention and sheepishly walked over. As soon as he was in reaching distance, Lynne wrapped us all together.

My chest ached. Blood thrummed in my eardrums. I was sure I was going to explode. But nothing happened. There was no massive destructive force or mysterious tornado. Just a family, my family, standing in a too small kitchen full of dirty dishes and crayon drawings.

EPILOGUE

I stared at the black leather-bound book filled with blank pages in front of me as I sat at the massive writing desk in the library. Alison was sprawled out under the willow tree beside me and the chirps of Olivia's game and Roland's mutters as he tried to help her beat the next level wafted through from the parlor across the hall. Somewhere in the back of the house, Lynne and Lydia prepared a 'not-quite-Christmas' slash 'official-adoption' feast.

The journal, a present from Lydia, felt daunting. Like my life wasn't quite as interesting as the ones documented in the diaries filling the bookshelf beside me. But, as my duty as a Blessed Sister, I'd fill the pages anyway. Maybe somehow, in some distant future, one of my descendants would need my story, just like I had needed Dawn's and Anne's.

If I was just a little more like Lydia and believed in a great plan, maybe I would think all of this was for a reason. That we were supposed to learn to help guide future generations. But I was still a bit too cynical for grand designs and destined fates. Still, I didn't want to risk it.

I didn't want someone else to get lost and not be able to find their way back because I didn't hold up my end of the deal.

I would be better than my grandmother. I would leave breadcrumbs.

So I went all the way back to where things began in order to tell the tale of how the Lost Daughter came back.

My hands shook, but just barely, as I wrote with the fine tipped pen that came with the journal.

"I knew better than to get comfortable here. But I'd let myself slip."

ACKNOWLEDGMENTS

I was sixteen years-old when I first heard the D word. I'd known something was wrong. Life wasn't fun any more. I mean, sure, my friends we're awesome and I had every reason to be happy. But I just wasn't. I constantly felt like there the weight of the entire world was on my shoulders. Like I wasn't enough. Like I'd *never* be enough. And I kept it all in, letting my friends see little tiny waves of the massive ocean roiling beneath the surface. One of them eventually told my mom. I was forced to go to a counselor. And she told me I had clinical depression. That I *was* good enough. That the chemicals in my brain we're just a little off. That we could fix it.

I was *so* mad at the time. I didn't want help. I just wanted to be "normal". It felt like they were saying I was broken. And while all those feelings are completely valid, I learned over the years as I grew up, that there is no normal. Everyone is fighting their own battles that you can't see. Mental health issues and Depression are 10000x more common than I knew back then.

Then my own kids were born. Going through what I did as a kid and teen, I knew what signs to look for. They didn't have to go it alone until someone ratted on them. I got them help the moment the first signs of depression and mental health issues popped up. And for both of them, I've done my best to be a safe haven – even for the issues they have that I don't.

But I know that not every child has the luxury of parents who really understand. Some of them don't know what's happening in their own body.

That's why I wrote this book.

Avery has Depression. The darkness in her head isn't just a mystical source of power. It's a real illness that affects millions.

Her sister has ADHD and Anxiety. Where Avery's inky, blackness bleeds through her thoughts, Lydia's light magic *burns* through hers - often scattering them to far off places.

Which is why I'd like to thank each and every person in my life that's helped me get to a point to where I can not only *live* with my conditions, I can keep them controlled enough to write entire books about them.

To my late mother, who gave me a love of words, a soft heart, and the willpower to persevere.

To my father, who is living proof that once you give someone the tools to be an ally, they can surprise you every day. Thank you for learning and growing. Thank you for believing me and the kids when we tell you how things affect us. Thank you for watching out for Wildflower's wellbeing at every single turn. We are beyond blessed to call you ours.

To Sonshine, my doppleganger. I am so proud of you. Each and every day. You're my little cinnamon roll, even though you are taller and stronger than me. You make a pretty excellent human and your ability to care for others is immense. This will probably be the last book I put out before you graduate and go out on your own. So while you're out there, remember: never loose your softness, no matter how much the world tries to turn you into stone.

To Wildflower, my littlest ball of fire. You have taught me more about myself and more about life than you will ever know. I didn't even realize I was so impatient until I had to learn how to be patient with you. You've changed everyone's life around you. Everyone who meets you knows how incredibly special you are. Just remember that sometimes your brain is lying to you if it ever tells you any different.

To my RaeRae, the best friend a girl could ever ask for. I couldn't do any of this without you, but especially this part. You take my bad, you take my good, and you never complain. When my own days are dark, you are my light.

To Meh, who gave me all the low-down about Boston and drove me out to Salem just to help me release this book. The universe put you in my path and I will forever be grateful. Here's to being Co-Everythings forever.

To AayrBear, the non-reader who now reads everything. You turned your life completely upside down because you wanted to support me. You make me feel valid, important, and loved and I'll spend every day forever paying it back.

To Ali, JJ, Joz, and AU510, my bonus babies. I hope you know that my door is always open and my heart is always yours. When the darkness comes, you know where I am.

To Elle, our fearless leader, for putting up with me (and sometimes my little crew) through so much and opening the doors to MTP to me and my little witchy babes.

ABOUT AUTHOr

Laynie Bynum is a southern dreamer and author. She believes the the dark, twisty parts of us are the bits that make us unique and embracing them is the path to peace. When she's not writing or reading, she's lost in the wilderness with her kids somewhere in the Appalachian mountains, searching for their next great adventure.

COMInG SOON

Child of Light

Lydia Coal isn't certain of anything anymore. Not after finding out magic exists, she has a twin sister she's never known, and her parent's adopted her.

With the bees in her head threatening to take over, she's obsessed with finding her birth father, but as the reality she's known shatters she must uncover the truth of her past and learn how to heal before her own magic consumes her.

If you or someone you love has a hard time with their darkness like Avery, please reach out to someone.
Life is hard, but it's harder when we try to do it by ourselves.
If you don't know where to begin call 1-800-662-HELP any time day or night to connect to the SAMHSA's national helpline.
They can connect you to providers and services in your area.
There is no shame in having darkness, and even less in asking for help - just like Avery had to learn to do.

ALSO FROM MIDNIGHT TIDE

Their love for music sparked a curse...

Lark Espinoza could get lost in her music—and she's not so sure anyone in her family would even care to find her. Her trendy, party-loving twin sister and her mother-come-lately Beth, who's suddenly sworn off men and onto homemaking, don't understand her love of cassette tapes, her loathing of the pop scene, or her standoffish personality. For outcast Lark, nothing feels as much like a real home as working at Bubble's Oddities store and trying to attract the attention of the cute guy who works at the Vinyl shop next door—the same one she traded lyrical notes with in class.

Auden Ellis silences the incessant questions in his own head with a steady stream of beats. Despite the unconditional love of his aunt-turned-mother, he can't quit thinking about the loss of his parents—or the possibility he might end up afflicted with his father's issues. Despite his connection with lyric-loving Lark, Auden keeps her at arm's length because letting her in might mean giving her a peek into something dangerous.

When two strangers arrive in town, one carrying a mysterious, dark object and the other playing an eerie flute tune, Lark and Auden find that their painful pasts have enmeshed them in a cursed future. Now, they must come to terms with their budding attraction while helping each other challenge the reflection they see in the mirror. If they fail, they'll be trapped for eternity in a place beyond reality. Perfect for fans of Stranger Things and Pretty in Pink. Set in 1985, Lyrics & Curses is full of nostalgia, romance, mystery, and a story like no other.

Fight like a magical girl in this paperback original contemporary fantasy in which a Harajuku fashionista battles mutants-and social anxiety-by teaming up with an elite group of outcasts. Perfect for those obsessed with the technicolor worlds of *Sailor Moon*, *The Umbrella*

Academy, **and the Marvel Cinematic Universe. Book One of the Magic Mutants Trilogy.**

Holly Roads uses Harajuku fashion to distract herself from tragedy. Her magical girl aesthetic makes her feel beautiful-and it keeps the world at arm's length. She's an island of one, until advice from an amateur psychic expands her universe. A midnight detour ends with her vs. exploding mutants in the heart of San Francisco.

Brush with destiny? Check. Waking up with blue blood, emotions gone haywire, and terrifying strength that starts ripping her wardrobe to shreds? Totally not cute. Hunting monsters with a hot new partner and his unlikely family of mad scientists?

Way more than she bargained for.

A portion of proceeds from this book will be donated to Heart Gallery Alabama.

Heart Gallery Alabama is a nonprofit organization dedicated to finding forever families for children in Alabama's foster care system by raising awareness and educating the public. For more information on who they are and how you can help, please visit HeartGalleryAlabama.com.